The POWER *of* LOVE *and* FEAR

Finding Faith in the
Midst of Betrayal,
Abandonment,
and Addiction

JANICE ELIZABETH BIMM

Printed in Canada

ISBN: 978-1-4866-1208-6

Word Alive Press
131 Cordite Road, Winnipeg, MB R3W 1S1
www.wordalivepress.ca

WORD ALIVE
—P R E S S—

MIX
Paper from
responsible sources
FSC
www.fsc.org   FSC® C016245

Cataloguing in Publication information may be obtained through Library and Archives Canada

Dedicated to my Lord and Saviour.

ACKNOWLEDGEMENTS

To my friends and family. A special thanks to Samantha Brands for helping me complete my dream in publishing this book, and to Jaymi Hallows and Sara Flint for the ongoing, unbelievable emotional support throughout my lifetime.

THE POWER OF LOVE AND FEAR
PROLOGUE

She knew that there were no short cuts when dealing with emotional pain, and that there were no short cuts to any place worth going. If she wanted to be free from the pain inflicted on her, and the pain she'd caused herself, she would have to be diligent in her prayer life, swallow her foolish pride, and ask for help. If she didn't deal with the core issues in her life, she would repeat the same patterns over and over again, and nothing would change.

As a client in an addictions program, she was encouraged to write about her pain and anger. A counsellor explained to her that if she were serious about her recovery, she would have to work with them, because she was only as sick as the secrets she was keeping locked away inside of her. If she persisted in refusing help, she would never know what God's grace-filled path for her life was. At first she adamantly refused to participate in that exercise, but when her counsellor persisted, she gave in and learned that there was merit in getting her true feelings out on paper.

When she finally sat down to write, she struggled to be honest with herself. Maybe things weren't as bad as she thought they were; perhaps she just wasn't emotionally mature enough to handle life's storms. In the end, her persistence paid off. Once she started writing, she was amazed at how quickly the words flowed onto the paper. She'd never shared those feelings with anyone before. It was an empowering experience for her.

At her next counseling session, her counselor told her that she was proud of her because of the courage it took to dig deep into her soul and bring light to those hidden feelings. After many counseling sessions, she'd come to realize that fear and anger were the underlying emotions that had driven her for many years.

What was she so afraid of? Why had she allowed fear to rule her? It would take years of prayer and work to find the answers to those questions.

Her fear and anger didn't instantly go away just because she wrote about and shared those long lost feelings. Even the day she was discharged from the rehab program, she was still filled with the fear that she wouldn't fit back into society or be accepted. She was afraid that her husband wouldn't understand how important it was that she continue to work on the program to stay sober, and how necessary it would be for them as a couple to travel the road together. Had the rehab center not given her a box full of "tools" with which to start her new life, she never would have known that she didn't have to let fear rule her anymore. Her plan had been to overcome and to understand why she'd abused alcohol and been willing to destroy her life. Was she not worth saving?

Her journey, however, hadn't gone as planned. By the grace of God, she'd been able to ride out the storms, and now twenty-five years later, she knew that the journey had been worth it. For the first time in her life, she could honestly say she was free. She was living proof that on the other side of her wall of fear, freedom awaited her if she was willing to trust God and acknowledge Him in all her ways.

PREAMBLE

Her relatives were God fearing, kind people who worked exceptionally hard to provide for their families. They came from a time in history when no one talked about their feelings; instead, they were taught to hide those emotions and be ashamed and afraid of them. If they revealed how they really felt, they may be looked upon as weak. Lying in a puddle of tears in the corner for the entire world to see was not an option.

This was an unwritten code in her family home; it was practically instinctive. She was expected to stuff her feelings deep inside and carry on presenting a strong exterior to the world. She never begrudged them for their inability to "talk feelings," because she believed it was a learned behavior passed down from generation to generation.

She desired to break that generational curse by telling her story so that the next generation would know there's no shame in talking about their pain. On the contrary, it takes courage to talk openly and honestly about whatever pain and fear you may be carrying in your heart. In the Bible we're told to carry each other's burdens (Galatians 6:2). If we keep our burdens a secret, we can't expect someone to read our heart or mind and offer their prayers, love, and support to help us heal.

When we hide pain deep within us in an attempt to avoid dealing with it, we open the door to fear. Fear is not from God, but from Satan (2 Timothy 1:7). Fear paralyzes us and causes us to make bad choices, and we have to live out the consequences of those choices. We aren't the only ones that will suffer, because what we do will have a cumulative effect on everyone and everything around us—our families, our friends, our finances, our health, and our relationship with God. All these can be destroyed when we start a chain reaction that causes the whole house of cards to fall. The only one who will be rejoicing is Satan, because he likes nothing better than to watch us destroy ourselves and take many down with us.

Satan is alive and well and isn't just a cartoon character with a red suit and a pitch fork. It's impossible to defeat our enemy if we refuse to believe he exits. Satan also knows that it's impossible for us to give or receive love when we are consumed with fear. The opposite of fear isn't war, but peace. When peace rules in our hearts, we can stand unmoved against the evil around us. The only way we find the peace that passes all understanding is by walking with God, because He is love (John 4:8).

Human beings posses two major emotions—love and fear. All other emotions are a variation of these two. Our thoughts and behavior come from either a place of love or a place of fear. There was no doubt in her mind that ever since the age of eight her fear had won out over love in the life choices she made. She was a fake. Her feelings didn't match her behavior, and her insides didn't match her outer appearance. On the outside she was smiling, but on the inside she was hurting and scared to death that people wouldn't like her. What had happened to her at the age of eight that caused her to take sixty years to fully comprehend the power that love and fear had?

Her fears were real when it came to writing her story. If she used the characters' real names, it would look like she was out for revenge and trying to shame the people who'd hurt her. That may have felt good for a moment, but she didn't want to come across as judging the people in her life. In her drinking days, she judged plenty of people and would always find a way to justify her behavior. She'd wanted life to run according to her plans, as though someone had put her on a pedestal at the center of the universe, and everyone was supposed to do whatever she wanted.

The rehab center had really done a number on her. They expected her and all the other clients in the program to start living and breathing the Twelve Step Program they talked about constantly. She tried to do what was asked of her, but the more she studied the twelve steps, the more afraid she became. What would happen to her if she couldn't walk the walk? She was scared to death she wouldn't be able to make amends or forgive the people who'd hurt her. What if she lived out the rest of her days with unforgiveness in her heart?

If she were placed in a coffin and still had unforgiveness in her heart, that would mean she'd lived a miserable life. Everyone she'd come in contact with would have taken a hit because of her wounded, unforgiving spirit. By the time she was in her coffin it would be too late. She wouldn't be able to crack open the lid and yell, "Hey, you over there ... tell so and so I forgive them." She'd take her wounded spirit with her into eternity, and she wasn't willing to risk doing that.

She also needed to hold herself accountable for the role she played in relationships. It wasn't always the other guy's fault. Was there anyone left on her list that she needed to ask to forgive her, and then to try to make amends with? She'd been diligent with her efforts to do the best she could with what life had given her, because she didn't want to be holding anyone hostage in her mind or heart when she left this world.

She knew people, including members of her own family, living with unforgiveness in their hearts and masters at disguising their pain. They seemed to be under the power of a deep rooted fear, and their fear came across as anger. In the past whenever she talked openly about her faith, Twelve Step programs, the importance of prayer, or what she believed God expected from her, she felt that others viewed her as self-righteous. In fact, her second husband told her that although she had good intentions, she scared people off and made them feel inferior to her when she talked about faith, change, and recovery. He told her to let people come to her. When he said that, she concluded that he must be ashamed of her for talking out loud about matters that were near and dear to her heart.

His words contradicted everything she learned in her program and from the Bible. She knew that she'd been given much, and that much was expected of her. She continued to share her story with anyone who wouldn't run away from her. Just because her husband didn't want to hear it didn't mean that she should just sit back and knit a sweater or take up golfing while she waited for someone to show up at her door.

Many scriptures clearly state that true saving faith results in a transformed life, which is demonstrated by the work we do. Faith without works is a dead faith, because the lack of works reveals an unchanged life or a spiritually dead heart. The truth was she didn't feel self-righteous … she felt afraid. Her fear wasn't the unhealthy and paralyzing kind she'd felt after being betrayed. This fear was empowering, because it was rooted in her faith. She knew it was healthy to "fear the Lord," because it was the road to wisdom, salvation, and eternal life. One of her favorite quotes was by Ralph Waldo Emmerson: "The wise man in the storm prays to God, not for safety from danger, but for deliverance from fear. It is the storm within that endangers him, not the storm without."

Only time would tell if what she professed to believe matched how she lived. Had God delivered her from her fear? Had the storm inside of her finally been calmed? Would her feelings be in harmony with her behavior? It would be hypocritical of her to say she was a Christian and an alcoholic in recovery if she didn't act like one.

***

This story is dedicated to my Lord and Savior. He never promised me smooth sailing, but He did promise me a safe landing. The sailing hasn't always been smooth, and I've found myself in the midst of some turbulent waters. When I was at my worst and filled with fear, He picked me up and carried me and calmed the storm brewing inside of me. Without Jesus in my life I am nothing. I am eternally grateful that He saved me.

1

Two Strikes…
You're Hopeless!

Lauren couldn't recall anyone ever asking for her forgiveness. She'd heard "I'm sorry" and "no harm intended," but never had a real, genuine apology been offered to her, and no one had ever made amends to her.

She was sixty-eight years old and had two ex-husbands. When she was twenty-seven, Doug, her husband of seven years, handed the keys and the mortgage of their home over to her and said he was leaving. The day he left he threw $20.00 down on the counter.

"I'm taking the farm and the bank account," he announced. "You get the house. And by the way, you're going to need a car because you'll have to go back to work, so I bought you a used one."

With those words hanging in the air, he turned and walked out the door and didn't even say "I'm sorry."

When Lauren was sixty-two years old, Matt, her second husband, handed the keys of the house over to her.

"I'm sorry I ruined your life," he said while looking at the floor.

They'd been married for twenty-three years, but had been together for twenty-six. As she watched Matt walk out the door forever, Lauren fired back at him.

"You can't say you ruined my life … you don't have the power to, because you don't own me. Your actions and words destroyed my life as I knew it, and you changed the course of my life, but I'm the only one who can ruin it."

Both husbands committed adultery and abandoned her. In the days that followed both betrayals, Lauren suffered greatly. Adultery killed her spirit, and she was left feeling unwanted, unloved, ugly, and useless. During those times, she often wondered what it must have been like for Jesus when Judas betrayed Him. He hadn't been blindsided, because He knew that one of His disciples would betray Him. That would make it even worse—knowing beforehand that one of your friends was going to turn their back on you. That betrayal resulted in Jesus hanging on a cross, which for mankind offered the hope of eternal life. Jesus suffered so that we could live with the hope of eternal life in our hearts.

Lauren wasn't comparing her suffering to Jesus' suffering, but she wondered if she paid her story forward, would it help anyone to know that there was hope for them, and that they too could heal after being betrayed.

In the years that followed the end of her marriages, Lauren convinced herself that she was neither needed nor loveable, a feeling reinforced and validated by her second betrayal. Her first husband had ripped her heart wide open, and it took endless hours of work and prayer to forgive him and to heal and trust again. It was as if the second betrayal ripped the bandages off, causing her heart to gush blood for the second time. Then there were the voices that kept whispering in her ear: "You're no good … you couldn't have children and you're not smart enough or sexy enough for any man to be with you … that's why both men cheated on you and abandoned you. It's your fault."

Lauren secretly suspected that satanic forces somehow cheered on those voices in her head. She dared not tell anyone, because she was sure they'd think she was drinking again, or that she was delusional and psychotic. When the voices became overwhelming, Lauren would get down on her knees and scream: "Devil, get out of here in the name of Jesus Christ!" That helped turn the volume down and provided her with some kind of relief from all that noise in her head.

She believed there was a war going on in the heavens and that it was her responsibility to choose what side she wanted to be on. When she was a teenager at Bible camp, one of her favorite songs had been "Onward Christian Solders." It spoke about marching on to war with the cross of Jesus in the lead. That meant that she needed to wear her spiritual armor at all times if she planned to march for Jesus. She also believed that the devil knew full well that without her armor on, she would be nothing more than a pawn in his dirty game. She didn't want to be anyone's pawn. She wanted to fight the good fight wearing the strongest and best armor possible.

That all sounded honorable, but the problem was the devil had her number. He knew what would bring her to her knees and see her rip off her spiritual armor and throw it into the corner to collect dust. The problem was her pride. It has been said that pride is the right hand of Satan at work, and when Lauren stood looking both betrayals straight in the eye, her pride became wounded and she opened the door to evil. Wounded pride is one of the most dangerous evils known to mankind, and the spiritual war in which she had enlisted became the biggest fight of her life. It felt like the battle had moved from the heavens into her mind.

During that time in her life, she wondered what role the devil had played when Judas made the decision to betray Jesus. What voices had been whispered in his ear? Had he taken off his spiritual armor just long enough for the devil to sneak in and wound his pride, too?

2

THE MESSENGER

Lauren sat at a table with her head down so that she didn't have to make eye contact with anyone. She was crying and feared that someone would see her that way. What was wrong with her? What was a girl like her doing in a treatment center for alcohol abuse? She came from a good family, had a great job, was married, and lived in a beautiful home on the lake. What a disgrace it was that she ended up in a treatment center. It was a place for losers … the kind of guys you see on the streets passed out with a brown paper bag in their hand. She didn't need to be there. She was better than that, and as soon as she could think straight, she'd leave.

While in the process of trying to figure out an escape route, she heard footsteps coming in her direction. She quickly put her face on the tear stained table and folded her arms over her head. She heard the footsteps stop right at her table.

"Hi," a sweet, calm voice said. "I'm Pat. My husband is in the program with you. Here, this is for you. Good luck."

Lauren mumbled a thank you, but when she finally looked up, there was no one else in the room with her. Where had that woman come from? Where had she gone to? It was obvious that someone had been there, because a business card lay on the table in front of her.

On the front of the card was a picture of a kite, and written in bold letters were the words, "Hang in There (Proverbs 3:5)." Handwritten on the back were the words, "Trust in the Lord with all thine heart; and lean not unto thine own understanding. In all thy ways acknowledge

Him, and He shall direct thy paths." In bold letters were written the words "Pass It On."

At that moment in time Lauren had no idea the impact that little card would have in her life. As the years rolled by, she often referred affectionately to that time as her "Big Grace Moment." There was no doubt in her mind or heart that she experienced divine intervention that day. If she'd known then what the future held for her, she never would have believed it. In the years that followed, whenever she was in the darkest and deepest valleys of her life, she experienced more moments of grace that would change the course of her life forever. It was as if her whole life had been orchestrated with purpose.

3

HURRY UP...
PICK ONE

Lauren and Matthew married on Friday, July 13, at 7:00 p.m. in a quaint little church next door to an apartment building Matt lived in as a child. A minister officiated at the wedding service. There were five people in the wedding party: Lauren's best friend, Christina, Matt's two brothers, Murray and Mark, and the bride and groom. No guests were invited. The event had been shrouded in secrecy because Lauren had been married before, and she didn't want to make a big deal out of this wedding.

She hadn't told anyone in her family about the wedding, because her mother was ill and things were in a mess at her parent's home. Her mother was suffering immensely with brain damage caused by a brain tumor, and her father began to drink to excess. Lauren tried to hold him accountable, but this resulted in heated arguments that would end with no resolution. Ironically, the "pot was calling the kettle black," because both Lauren and her father tried to drink their pain away. Since her dad didn't know how much she was drinking, she felt like she had the upper hand and could chastise him for drinking too much.

Prior to the wedding, Matt and Lauren lived together in the home she managed to hang to after her first husband did his disappearing act. The odd thing was that Matt still paid rent on an apartment across the lake, even though he never used it. It was as though he had a backup plan just in case things didn't work out.

Two months before the wedding as Matt was leaving for work he yelled: "Hey Lauren, call a minister today or I'm out of here!" With that he slammed the door. Lauren could still remember the sick feeling she had in her stomach when she heard those words. Matt's ultimatum left her feeling like a caged animal.

As she paced back and forth in the kitchen, beads of sweat formed on her forehead, so she opened the freezer door and stuck in her head. She felt like she was going to pass out, but the cool air revived her. She grabbed a bottle of water and went out onto the deck. The view was spectacular. The lake was calm and serene, and she felt herself beginning to relax and settle down. She desperately wanted to have a drink, but it was only 10:00 a.m. and she'd promised herself that she wouldn't drink before noon. At 12:01, she poured herself a shot of brandy.

Decades later, she could still remember the battle that raged inside of her that day. What to do? Call a minister and book a wedding date, or risk Matt leaving her? If he left her, she'd be alone again, and that thought petrified her. Also, it would be easier if she had someone with whom to share her financial burden. Best of all, she could "save face" by having a younger, handsome man by her side. That would send a message to the world that she was needed and loved ... and maybe if a miracle happened, she could get pregnant and become the mother she so desperately wanted to be.

When her first husband cheated on and abandoned her, she felt unloved and not needed; she struggled to find a job and keep her home. She had some good survival skills, but when it came to fixing things like a leaky roof, a malfunctioning septic system, an old furnace, or her car, she was lost. She had to beg someone to help her so that she wouldn't have to break the bank just to remain in her home.

After a few shots of brandy, Matt gave her the ultimatum and she decided to move forward with the marriage. Her fear of being alone surpassed her fear of getting married again. In reality, she picked the lesser of two fears. In years to follow, she wondered what Matt would have done had the tables been turned and he'd been given the same ultimatum.

By the time Matt came home from work, Lauren had called a minister. Unfortunately, his Saturdays were booked until the fall, but he could marry them on a Friday evening in July. It just happened to be

Friday the thirteenth. Was she superstitious? She assured him she wasn't, and told him she would call him back after she talked to the groom.

She was a little tipsy when she gave Matt the news about the wedding date.

"Okay then," he responded, "let me get a cold beer and we'll have a toast."

By the time they went to bed that night there was no beer (Matt's drug of choice) left, and Lauren's bottle of brandy (her drug of choice) was just about empty. And so began their journey towards matrimony.

4

TWO FUNCTIONING
ALCOHOLICS SAY "I DO"

The groom got three hours of sleep the night before the big day, because he'd been out celebrating his up and coming wedding with a girl he knew from his high school days. When he arrived home at 3:00 a.m., he woke Lauren up and told her that he'd just happened to run into his old friend and her sister at Jimmy's (the local sports bar).

When he dragged himself out of bed at 7:00 the next morning to go to work, he looked and stank like he was still drunk. Lauren didn't look or smell much better, because she too had been drinking the evening before while she was alone at home. It wasn't okay with her to have the world see her drunk. If no one witnessed her getting drunk, she was fooling them. She knew how to force a smile, even when she was dying on the inside. In fact, she became so good at hiding her drinking that not even those closest to her suspected that she would soon crash.

The wedding party arrived at the church five minutes before the ceremony was to take place. When Matt had arrived home from work that day, he'd jumped into the lake to cool off, which left him with little time to dress. He hadn't been able to find his black shoes, so he'd polished his brown shoes black, and then threw on his clothes and broke the speed limit getting to the church on time. The minister was waiting for them at the front of the church. With no guests sitting in the pews, no flowers, and no wedding music, the sanctuary didn't look or sound like a wedding was about to take place.

The wedding party lined up in front of the minister, and the ten minute ceremony began. The young clergyman read from 1 Corinthians

13:4–8 and briefly spoke on the biblical meaning of love. The bride and groom exchanged rings and kissed, and the wedding was over. They signed a few papers, and when they turned to exit the church, Lauren had a sinking feeling in her stomach. She'd never been in a church when all the pews were empty. There were no people waiting to hug or congratulate them … what a disappointment. What had she been thinking when she insisted the wedding be kept a secret? Was she ashamed that she was marrying a second time? Why did she think that she didn't deserve a second chance … because she was damaged goods? Who had made her feel that way?

She did have proof that some people considered her damaged. After her relationship with Matt began, her friend, Bruce, arranged a date for her with his cousin, Allan. Lauren hadn't been interested, but finally gave in when Bruce kept insisting that she at least try to have some fun. When Allan called her, she agreed to go out to dinner with him.

During dinner while the two of them talked about their families, he mentioned that his mother was very upset with him and had warned him to stay away from divorced women. She said that she hated them because they were damaged, money hungry woman, and even the church frowned upon them. For that reason alone the mother hadn't wanted her thirty-seven year old, single son to be anywhere close to one of those women. If he got involved with a divorced woman, it would bring great shame to their family.

Lauren felt relieved when that date ended. She'd felt like telling Allan to make sure that when he got to his mommy's house, he told her that he'd stoned that money hungry divorced woman to death. Maybe that would cheer her up. Needless to say, she never dated Allan again.

The "take away message" that date left with Lauren was that she was damaged goods, and nobody, not even the church, would want anything to do with her. When Matt moved in with her six months later, he validated and reinforced this message. After coming home from visiting his parents, he said that when he and his father were talking about her, his dad scolded him and told him that he could have done better. This hurt Lauren deeply, and she wondered why Matt shared that information with her. Was he insensitive, or had he said it to hurt her so he could have the upper hand?

Years later, Lauren wondered if Matt had been raised hearing the words, "You're not good enough ... do better." If so, one more "do better" would validate what he already believed about himself. He wasn't good enough, and no one had to remind him of it. She and Matt never spoke about his fathers' comment again.

Maybe Matt was no different than Lauren. She never forgot those "you're not good enough" messages, because they validated what she believed about herself. After all, she hadn't been good enough for her first husband. If Matt felt the same way she did, then two "not good enough," functioning alcoholics had just said "I Do." What a bleak future that presented.

At that time in her life, she remained true to the family code encrypted in her mind and heart. She stuffed those emotions and presumed that was the end of them; however, it wasn't over. The emotions kept sneaking out from under the rug and permeated her whole being. At her worst, the voices were the loudest. It was almost like they were chanting: "You have lots of proof that you aren't enough; nobody will ever love or need you."

It was enough to drive her insane, until she finally found a way to turn the volume down. With each drink she poured for herself, the voices sounded further and further away, until she heard nothing because she'd passed out. When she awoke with her head in the toilet, the voices returned with great intensity, except this time they were chanting: "You're an idiot. You're a fool. Only losers wake up with their head in the toilet."

Fortunately, on the day of the wedding Lauren didn't feel hung over. She knew that Matt was very hung over, because she could still smell the distinct odor of old beer on his breath. She knew that odor well, because her dad often smelled the same way. She always remembered her father having a pocket full of wintergreen Life Savers. Before walking into church, he'd pop two into his mouth. Was he trying to disguise the smell of beer on his breath? Maybe, unknown to her, his excessive drinking went back much farther than she realized.

The only thing different about the bride and groom that day as they exited the church were their shiny new wedding bands that had just been blest. Years later when Lauren noticed that Matt wasn't wearing the ring anymore, she asked him why he wasn't wearing it. He told her that management at work had recently told the employees that they couldn't wear rings when working with heavy duty equipment. It was a health and safety issue. When she asked him what he'd done with it, he opened his shirt and there it was, hanging around his neck on a gold chain. She believed his story that day, but it all changed a year later when the truth finally wormed its way out of him.

After twenty-two years of marriage, Lauren found herself in the same sanctuary where she and Matt had been married. On this occasion, she was on her knees at the altar with tears streaming down her face. All she could manage to get out was, "Help me ... please dear Jesus ... help me. It's happened again, and I'm so afraid." Once again, all the pews were empty and no music was playing. There was complete and total silence, except for the voices screaming inside her head.

The voices continuously repeated the same words: "I warned you. You're no good. He replaced you with a younger, prettier woman who makes him happy. Did the same thing your first husband did. Do you believe me now that you know he's betrayed you and you're alone again? Why don't you go get yourself a bottle of brandy? Don't forget that you started your drinking career after your first husband abandoned you for another woman. You'd be foolish to think that you can stay sober throughout this ordeal."

Lauren remained on her knees in the church for a long time. Before leaving, she offered up a prayer as she tried to wipe her tears off the communion rail. She didn't want to leave a permanent stain on that highly polished piece of sacred wood.

That day as she looked at the cross on the altar she recited: "Trust in the Lord with all thine heart, and lean not unto thine own understanding. In all thy ways acknowledge Him, and He shall direct thy paths." She then prayed: "Please direct my path, dear Lord. I'm scared to death that I'll drink again and kill Matt and his girlfriend. Thank you. In your precious son Jesus' name. Amen."

By the time she returned to her car, she figured out where the nearest liquor store was. It hadn't been the first time in her life that she'd been on a road that led to a liquor store and a church. Memories came flooding back about the day she'd run right past a liquor store in search of a church with an unlocked door.

5

LET THE PARTY BEGIN

Prior to the wedding, Lauren had made reservations at a Greek restaurant for a party of five. The group eagerly rushed in the door, and before they were seated in their chairs, the waitress was pouring ouzo into shot glasses on the table. Kate, Mark, and Murray raised their glasses and toasted the bride and groom with an "Opa!" Everyone in the restaurant chimed it.

The group wined and dined until closing time. Lauren knew the owners of the restaurant, so they were served the best food and liquor that money could buy. No one in the wedding party wanted the celebration to be over.

One of Matt's brothers suggested that they stop by Jimmy's Sports Bar before heading home. Everyone agreed, and fifteen minutes later they were walking into Jimmy's. All the locals were there, and someone yelled, "Hey, listen up. Lauren and Matt just got married. If you feel like buying the bride and groom, the best men, and the maid of honor a drink, come this way, please."

The liquor began to flow like it was free, and even the guys who'd been watching a hockey game or throwing darts found their way to the bar to congratulate the lovely couple. Somebody took a picture of the bridal party with each person holding a different sized beer glass. That same picture ended up on display in Jimmy's bar for years to come.

Around midnight, Lauren decided to call her brother, Warren, and her good friend, Bruce, to tell them the good news and ask them to join them at the bar to help celebrate. Within fifteen minutes, Bruce and his wife, Marion, walked through the door, but her brother never showed. When she had spoken to him on the phone, he didn't sound happy and he asked why she had married without telling anyone in their family. Lauren never answered that question. When the news of Matt's affair broke years later, she called Warren and asked him for their father's gun. Her dad had used that gun for partridge hunting. He'd taught her gun safety, and even how to fire his .410. Her brother asked why she wanted it, so she told him that Matt was moving to an apartment, and she was afraid to stay alone. She'd feel safer if she knew she had a gun in the house.

Her brother reluctantly delivered it to her the next day and made her promise not to do anything stupid with it. Warren knew all about her temper. Years before, when she'd been drinking, he and Matt carried her into the house kicking and screaming because a neighbor had cut down a tree on the adjoining property line. Lauren had been enraged, because the guy had promised that he wouldn't cut it down. Liquor had fueled that fire in her that day, and it took a major hangover to make her realize how drunk and stupid she'd looked.

That same gun eventually became the topic of discussion at an A.A. meeting she attended a week after Matt had moved out. During her turn to speak, she described how hurt she was to find out about her husband's affair. She made some smart comment about getting her father's gun out because she'd been so enraged, but fortunately she stopped short of telling them she'd put a bullet in it and pointed it at her husband.

After the meeting, an elderly gentleman approached her and asked if he could talk to her. He introduced himself as Harry W.

"Sure," Lauren said reaching out her hand, "I can use all the help I can get."

He proceeded to tell her about a better way to deal with her anger than trying to resolve it with a gun in her hand.

"You could pray for the person that has wronged you, and ask God to bless them," he said in a quiet voice.

Lauren remained silent for a few moments, unable believe what she'd just heard. In a loud voice she said, "You have to be kidding me... you mean to tell me that if your wife cheated on you, you'd drop to your knees and pray for her and ask God to bless her?"

"Yes, that's exactly what I'd do," Harry responded, "after I had time to recover from the initial shock. I needed to talk to you, Lauren, because I could hear the fear and anger in your voice as you shared with the group. It sounds to me like you're so enraged that you're going to do something that you'll regret for the rest of your life. Do you know that the Bible tells us that vengeance is the Lord's? If you set out looking for revenge, you'll have to dig three graves before you leave home. You won't have to worry about ruining your husband's and his girlfriend's lives, because you'll be too busy ruining your own, and you'll drink again. That's the way this program works. You've got many years of sobriety under your belt. What's that worth to you?"

Lauren didn't say much after Harry finished talking; she just reached out her arms and gave him a huge bear hug. Before leaving the building, she looked at him and thanked him for saving her from a fate worse than death.

"You're welcome," Harry said. "Keep coming back." And she did.

She wasn't looking forward to getting home after that meeting, because there would be no one there but her dog. All Matt's belongings were gone. It had been sheer agony for her when she'd opened the medicine cabinet to get her toothbrush. As she put toothpaste on her brush, she experienced major déjà vu. She had experienced the same feeling of dread after her first husband took his belongings out of their home and she'd opened the medicine cabinet and found it half empty. It was as if something irreversible had taken place ... it was final. Doug wasn't coming back home.

Thirty-five years later the feelings were just as strong, but this time it wasn't Doug that wasn't coming home; it was Matt. Once again she reminded herself of how much easier it would have been if both husbands had died instead of running off with other women. At least then she would have been the one to remove their toothbrushes from the medicine cabinet instead of dealing with the shame and insanity that followed closely on the heels of a betrayal.

6

ANYBODY SEEN MATT?

The owner of Jimmy's kept the bar open for an extra hour the evening the wedding party crashed his place. When he insisted that everyone leave, the stragglers were reluctant to go. Matt suggested that everyone in the bar follow him and his bride to their house so that they could all go for a swim to sober up. Everyone agreed that was an excellent idea, and within moments the bar emptied.

Matt and Lauren hopped into their car and sped down the highway. Matt drove so erratically that his wife of six hours suggested that she should drive. She'd been drinking too, but guessed that she was a little less inebriated than he. He adamantly refused and kept driving until they came to the ballpark located less than a mile away from their home. He jumped out of the car, opened the trunk, grabbed a baseball bat, and started running around the bases while swinging the bat in the air yelling, "I'm married, I'm married."

After watching him do at least ten laps around the baseball diamond, Lauren yelled at him to get into the car so that they could go home to the people waiting to party with them for the rest of the night. He got into the passenger seat and off they went to the place that would be their marital home for the next nine years.

Matt's brothers were waiting in the driveway when they arrived home. When they asked what had taken them so long to get there, Lauren described her husband's antics at the ballpark. Mark grabbed Lauren by the hand, and Murray grabbed Matt, and the brothers led them across the front lawn, stopping in front of what looked like a big rock.

In the middle of their lawn sat a huge boulder. Matt's brothers shone a flashlight on it, revealing a long chain that was secured to it with a piece of metal on the other end that looked like a fetter one might use on a horse. It had a lock on it. The brothers grabbed Matt, closed the fetter and the lock around his ankle, and gave the key to Lauren.

Those gathered around raised their glass and toasted the groom. He was locked up; he couldn't go any further than the chain allowed him to, so he sat on the boulder, looking like he was going to pass out. Lauren kissed the top of his head and told him she would come back soon and unlock him.

Hours had passed before anyone noticed that Matt was missing.

"Hey you bunch of drunks," Mark yelled. "Anybody know where Matt's gone to?" Lauren jumped up with a smirk on her face.

"Oh no—I was supposed to go and unlock him hours ago. I've got the key in my pocket. I'll go set him free right now."

Lauren found Matt right where she'd left him on the lawn.

"Are you alright?" she asked him.

"I'm great ... except for the mosquito bites," he replied. "I think I'll go lie down."

She guided him to the spare bedroom; he was fast asleep by the time she was closing the door.

The party finally came to an end an hour later. Lauren did what she always did—cleaned up the mess and then fell into bed. When she opened her eyes the next morning, she felt like she'd been hit by a Mac truck. Matt didn't look much better, but he was out of bed and making coffee when she dragged herself into the kitchen. Together with coffee in hand, they went outside to have a look at the wedding boulder in the light of day.

The brothers had obviously put a lot of effort into decorating the wedding rock. It was so big that it would have been difficult for two men to carry it. On the face of the rock they had neatly painted in black: "Friday the 13th, 1989." The next line read: "Matt and Lauren." All around the edge of the rock they'd made a serious of black lines

Later that day Mark phoned to see how the newlyweds were doing, and he told them that on each anniversary, they were to paint a line through one of the black lines on the edge of the rock. He said it would be a good way to remember how many years they'd been married. On each anniversary that followed, Lauren got out her black paint and put a line through one of the marks on the rock. Oddly enough, those black lines began to look like a bunch of little crosses on the face of the rock. If only both of them had realized that those crosses could have saved their marriage … if only they had the willingness and the faith to believe in something greater than themselves.

7

WHY,
OH WHY?

The first seven years of their marriage went by quickly. Both Matt and Lauren remained functioning alcoholics. They managed to go to work every day and appear relatively normal, and their home became a drop in center for many of the locals in the area. They never knew who was going to show up at the front or back door. They came by foot, car, boat, bike, and snow machine.

Warren had to drive right by their house on his way home, and he often stopped by. He seemed to have gotten over not being invited to his sister's wedding, and often when Lauren got home from work she'd find Warren and Matt sitting on the dock or in the garage having a beer.

Lauren's youngest brother Karl, fifteen years her junior, was also married and had two little girls. He often stopped by for a quick beer, and usually had his daughters in tow. Lauren couldn't be happier—she loved those girls as if they were her own.

Their home was surrounded by family. Her aunt and uncle lived across the street, her parents and youngest sister, Beth, lived only minutes away to the left of their home, and Matt's parents and grandparents and Warren and his family and another aunt and uncle on Lauren's side lived only minutes away to the right. Karl and his family lived across the lake from them, and they knew just about everyone else in between, because both of them at been raised in the area.

At the rustic bar in their basement you could find many bottles of liquor with a person's name written on the front of the bottle and a black mark depicting where the owner of the bottle had left off when they'd gone home. This insured that no one other than the owner of that bottle drank from it. All the drinkers at that bar felt confident that when they returned, they would still have some of their drug of choice left.

Lauren wasn't as trusting with her liquor: even if it had her name on the bottle, she had to be absolutely sure that when she needed her liquor, it would be there. She didn't even tell Matt where her stash was hidden. She always had an extra bottle of brandy hidden behind a large flour canister in a kitchen cupboard. No one other than her had any reason to go into that cupboard.

From the day her first husband, Doug, moved into that house there had been lots of alcohol available in their home. Doug had been employed by the local police force, and often he and a few of his peers could be found drinking at that rustic bar. By the time he'd run off with another woman, Lauren was sure that he fit the definition of an alcoholic. His father had been a serious drinker, as had Matt's father and her own father.

Matt once told her that he'd started drinking at age twelve. She suspected that Doug also drank before he turned sixteen. Growing up, Lauren never liked the smell or the taste of liquor, but it was present at every family party, and all of her family members, with the exception of one aunt and uncle, drank—some of them to excess.

Lauren's drinking career started later in life. She was twenty-seven when Doug ran off, and she experienced difficulty sleeping. A friend suggested she try having a nightcap to relax her before bedtime. She thought it may be a good idea, because she was deathly afraid to take any kind of pills. She wasn't just paranoid—she had good reason to fear any kind of mind altering drugs.

She worked three different shifts in a hospital as a medical laboratory technologist, and her home base was in the chemistry lab. Their reports were the ones the doctors in Emergency wanted quickly when a suspected overdose showed up at the hospital. Lauren couldn't even guess the number of overdose screens she had done in her thirty-six year career.

Night shifts were the worst. You knew you could count on at least two overdoses a night. Full moon nights were even worse. The ER would call the lab, and the techs would go flying up to draw blood and then scurry back to the lab to analyze it. On numerous occasions while at a patient's bedside, Lauren would note the bags of meds some patients came in with. She found this appalling. Where had those people gotten all those prescriptions from? Why had they overdosed? Could their lives be that terrible that they wanted to end it, and pills provided them with a convenient way to get the job done?

These experiences led Lauren to promise herself that she'd never take mind altering drugs. Prescription sleeping pills fit into that category, so they were out. That left alcohol. For some unknown reason, she chose to buy brandy ... maybe because of the higher alcohol content, or maybe she thought drinking brandy sounded classier than drinking beer.

At first she gagged when she tried to get a shot of brandy down, but she kept on trying and eventually started to enjoy it. As her friend had promised, it relaxed her and sleep finally came.

Lauren became so reliant on that drink before bed that one shot quickly became two. As a night shift worker, she fell into bed at different times of the day. She worked seven days in a row, followed by seven afternoons, and then seven nights. She filled her days off with normal household duties and trying to catch up on her sleep. Working nights was the most difficult shift. She arrived home at 8:00 a.m. and panicked because it was hard to go to sleep when the sun was shining. At those times she advanced from her usual two shots of brandy to a small glass full of brandy and ice.

Five years into Lauren's marriage, her fifty-two year old mother had a seizure at home. Fortunately, her father was there to revive her and she was rushed to the hospital where Lauren worked. After admitting her and conducting extensive testing, the doctors discovered a brain tumor that needed to be surgically removed.

Lauren had been on the night shift when her mom's test results came in. She came home from work that morning and slept a few hours before she awoke, anxious to find out if her mother had seen her doctor. She got dressed and headed back to the hospital.

When she got there, she found her mother sitting up in bed and talking to a familiar woman. It was her mom's friend, Marg, who went to the same church as her family. Lauren smiled politely and asked her mom if the results had come in.

Her mother turned her head in Lauren's direction.

"Yes," her mom replied, "the doctor said I have a brain tumor and I need surgery."

Before Lauren could get a word out, her mother turned to face Marg again and they picked up the conversation right where they had left off. They'd been talking about an upcoming bake sale at the church.

Lauren stood frozen to the spot; she couldn't move or talk. She had a million questions, but her mother didn't appear concerned about the seriousness of her condition. Marg looked at Lauren and saw her devastation.

"Your mom will be okay, Lauren," she said comfortingly. "All the people at the church will be praying for her and your family."

Lauren stayed in the room and stared out the window for another twenty minutes while her mother and Marg talked about who was going to make what for the bake sale and how much they should charge for each item. When Lauren couldn't stand another moment of idle chit chat, she excused herself and told her mother that she would see her later. She told her to call her before 11:00 p.m. if she needed anything and she would drop it off to her before her shift started. All her mom said in return was, "Okay, thanks."

Walking to her car, Lauren knew that she still had plenty of time to make it to the liquor store before it closed. There was no doubt in her mind that she needed a stiff drink in order to power nap before going to work.

When she arrived home she grabbed a medium sized glass and filled it with brandy. By the time she emptied it, she was contemplating calling in sick to work. It didn't take long before she poured herself another drink and then picked up the phone and called in sick. It was 5:30 in the afternoon, and she was on her way to a good high. She didn't even have to think about it; she just knew she was in no shape to report critical blood results, and if someone ratted on her and told management that she smelled like booze, she could lose her job.

Before unplugging the phone, she thought about calling her dad and brothers to see if they knew about what took place at the hospital that day. Instead, she poured herself another drink and fell into bed with visions of her mother's head being split wide open flashing before her eyes.

She felt unbearable guilt. Why hadn't she at least approached her mom in the hospital and held her tightly and professed how sorry she was to hear the news from her doctor? Why had she lied to get out of a night shift? She wasn't sick; she was drunk. Why didn't she call or go to see her dad, or her brothers, or her sister? Why did she and her family act like they didn't care about each other? Why didn't any of them ever cry or hug each other during difficult times? Where was everyone when she needed them? Was she the only one that cared? More than anything, however, she wondered why her mother didn't act like a mother. She knew how hard it would be for Lauren to hear that dreadful news. Why had she ignored her at the hospital that day? Why had she acted like she barely knew her?

The worst was yet to come...

8
JANUARY 3, 1989—
EXTREME COLD, EXTREME GRIEF

Matt was an avid downhill skier. Although Lauren didn't enjoy the sport, she did like to be outdoors more than anything else. A friend of theirs asked if they'd like to go with him on a three day ski adventure at a resort four hours away. He'd do the driving, and he had a discount card for one of the nice hotels close to the ski hill. They told him that they'd love to go.

Lauren worked both Christmas and New Years, and was excited to have five days off in a row. It would be nice to get out of town for a few days. On December 31, she visited her dad at his home. He asked her to go to the liquor store and get him a few bottles of rum. She reminded him that he didn't drink rum, because, as he'd told her, it made him "stupid."

"Just get it for me," he said. "Here's the money. I'm sure Warren and his buddies will be stopping by on their machines tonight to shoot a little pool with me, and I want to have some hard stuff for them. You better stop at the beer store too and get me an extra case of Red Cap. I don't want to run out of that either. Those young whippersnappers sure can drink."

To avoid an argument, Lauren reluctantly agreed to do it. She told him that she and Matt would be out of town for a few days, and said that she was going to visit her mom later that day and then get a few groceries for her trip. When she mentioned that she was going to the hospital to see her mom, her dad went to the kitchen and started cutting fruit up into small pieces.

"Wait ... just wait ... don't leave yet," he said to her. "I'm not going to the hospital today, so bring this fruit to mom and make sure you get me the biggest bottles of rum they have— not the small ones. You can keep the change."

She felt sorry for her dad. His life had been turned upside down, and chances were that her mother would never be able to return home. He was like a ship without a rudder and a compass. He'd been a hard rock miner and had just retired when her mom became sick. He was ten years older than her, and she'd still been working as an admitting clerk at one of the local hospitals. Their lives were drastically altered the day her mother had a seizure, never to return to the normal they had once known.

Her dad had tried to look after her mom at home, but it became an impossible task. After her surgery, Lauren's mother's cognitive functioning was greatly altered. She lost most of her English speaking skills and reverted back to her original language—Finnish. Her dad knew no Finn, which added to his burden as her caregiver. After she fell in the driveway of their home and broke her hip, she never walked again.

That day Lauren did what her father asked—she bought him two forty ounce bottles of rum and a case of beer, and she brought the fruit to her mother and wished her a Happy New Year and told her that dad would visit her the next day. She had been transferred from the hospital where Lauren worked to a long term care facility at a hospital only a mile away. It was a sad place to visit because everyone on that floor knew they would never go home. It was like they were living on death row, waiting for their number to be up.

Eventually her mother stopped speaking altogether. If asked to repeat something, she'd sometimes get the first syllable out but that was it. It was like her voice was trapped inside her own body. Lauren knew that her dad was suffering. She could see it in his eyes as he watched her mom suffer, unable to change what had happened to her. She had been a strong, healthy, and busy woman who had taken great pride in her family and church.

Every time Lauren went to visit her mom she felt powerless and sad. Like her dad, she couldn't change what had happened to her mom.

Acceptance for her had been one of the biggest roadblocks, because she had not yet learned how to accept the things she couldn't change. She soon came to believe that she and her dad would never be able to accept what had happened to her mom, because both of them, as typical alcoholics, tried to drink their pain away. Alcoholism really was a soul sickness.

After every visit with her mom, Lauren stopped by the hospital chapel to sit quietly for a moment or two. She didn't pray a lot, but she appreciated the welcome silence of the sanctuary. It seemed to calm her enough so that she could continue on without falling apart.

Every time she returned to her car in the parking lot, she stared up at the big cross that sat atop the hospital. Usually a raven was perched on that cross making a lot of racket, which Lauren believed was a warning to stay away from his territory. Within ten years that cross and the cross on the hospital where she worked would both be taken down in the name of progress. She felt sad when that happened, so she started keeping her eye on all the other building that had crosses on them. One by one they were quickly disappearing, and she wondered if they all ended up in the dump.

She eventually started her own "save the cross" collection. She wanted to see how many used crosses she could collect before getting old or senile. She planned to leave a note in her will for her nieces, asking them to put the saved crosses out on a table at her funeral with a note that said: "Need a Cross? Please Take One." Often while in a second-hand store she would spot a cross that someone had abandoned, so she'd buy it and shine it up when she got home. She didn't hold much hope that she could save a large cross on a building, but she could retrieve discarded personal crosses. As her collection grew, so did her hope that people would stop throwing their crosses away.

She wasn't thinking about crosses as she drove to her dad's with the supply of alcohol he'd ordered; instead, she was trying to decide whether or not to hold him accountable for the amount he was drinking. Pulling into the driveway she decided against it. Why ruin his New Year's Eve celebrations? She knew that Warren and many of his friends would visit him that night, and that Karl would probably join the group as well.

Her father's basement was a fun place to visit. It housed a wood burning stove in the corner across from a bar made out of pine. Her dad loved to challenge people to try to beat him at a game of their choice at his pool and ping pong tables. The refrigerator was always full of beer, and it was free for all who visited. Her dad had always preferred to be at home and have people come to him. Her brothers and their friends loved it there. It was a fun place, full of laughter and happy yelling. Often Lauren heard people yell, "Hey, you're playing dirty pool!" Lauren was familiar with that expression, because she'd heard her dad use it many times. He told her that it was a way to say that one's behavior was morally unclean, unfair, underhanded, or unsportsmanlike. Tragically, the basement that had been full of laughter, fun, and drinking would soon be silenced. Within forty-eight hours, the world would stop turning for Lauren and her siblings.

Matt and Lauren went on the ski trip with their friend, Jack. The weather looked promising for their first day of skiing. Shortly after arriving at the hill, Matt heard his name being paged over the loudspeaker. They wanted him to report to the main office.

"That's strange," he said to Lauren. "I don't even know anyone in this town."

Within five minutes he was back, looking like something was very wrong. He asked Lauren to take a walk with him.

"Right now … with my ski boots on?" she said.

He took her by the arm and they began to walk.

"Warren's been trying to reach us," he began. "I hate to tell you this, but your dad died."

"What do you mean?" Lauren gasped. "There's been a mistake … not my dad …oh no … not my dad."

Matt held her tightly. "I'm so sorry, Lauren. Your dad's neighbor, Barry, found him this morning in the snow bank at the back door of his house; it was minus forty last night. He was frozen with no sign of life. Barry called an ambulance, but nothing could be done."

The following days were nothing more than a big blur. Lauren's constant companion was a bottle of brandy. She no longer cared who saw her drunk. After her dad's funeral service, she stood at the door of the church as people exited.

"You need a Kleenex," her cousin whispered to her.

"I need way more than a Kleenex." she responded.

She didn't care if the whole world saw her with snot running down her face. Didn't they get it? The man who sang "You are the Sunshine of My Life" and "Beautiful, Beautiful Brown Eyes" to her was dead ... gone forever.

Between fits of crying, she felt tremendous guilt. She had no doubt that her dad had been drinking rum that night from the bottles she'd delivered to his door. Why had she let him convince her to get that rum and beer for him? His autopsy showed that he was five times over the legal limit. He would have been close to death from ethanol poisoning, so the alcohol coupled with the cold ended his life. At least he didn't suffer in the snow bank; he was so drunk that he just passed out. His death also saved him from watching his wife suffer for ten more agonizing years in hospital—never to return home.

Lauren returned to work a week after her father's death. Everyone told her it would be good for her, but they didn't have to work in a lab or open a refrigerator door that held their father's autopsy blood. She couldn't avoid opening that fridge door, because the reagents to run her equipment were stored in it. Every time she opened the door, it reminded her that her father had died a drunk in a snow bank. No dignity in that. Just like the homeless people you heard about that lived and died on the streets because they were drunk on antifreeze or mouthwash. She'd see them in ER fighting for their lives, and she took blood from them and analyzed it, but it rarely made any difference, because most of them would go from ER to the morgue in a short period of time.

Her dad didn't even make it to the ER; he went directly to the morgue, and then hopefully to Heaven. There was no doubt in her mind that he believed in God. He took her everywhere when she was a child, with the exception of work. Her favorite memories were of the two of them picking blueberries while he told her stories from the Bible. She knew all about Noah and the ark, and Joseph and his multicolored coat, and how brave David took on Goliath the giant with nothing more than a slingshot and his faith.

Her dad loved the birds of the Bible, especially the sparrow. He often told her that if God fed and looked after a tiny little sparrow, He would look after her, too. When their baskets were full, he'd look for a branch on a blueberry bush that was heavy laden with berries. He'd break that branch off, leave all the berries and leaves intact, and place it on the top of their full basket. The branch would be for her mother when they returned home.

9

WHEN DID YOU HAVE
YOUR LAST DRINK?

Someone had to tell her mother that her husband was dead. No one, not even the doctors, knew if she would comprehend the death of her husband. There had been no visible recognition on her part when people she knew went into her room. She would just stare blankly at them and not utter a word.

Lauren knew that she had to be the one to do it, so she called Doreen, an old friend of her mother's and a practicing lawyer. Lauren needed a power of attorney in order to take over and clean up the mess that was left behind. Their house would have to be sold, because her mom would never leave the hospital. The only will Lauren found gave her mother power of attorney for her dad and her dad power of attorney for her mother.

She arranged to meet Doreen at the hospital, and the two of them, hand in hand, entered her mother's room. Lauren held a Bible she'd received from members of the mining community at the funeral home. It was a beautiful, leather bound Bible with her dad's name engraved on it. She took her mother's frail hand in hers and asked if she recognized Doreen, but her mother's expression didn't change. Lauren placed the Bible at her mother's side and explained that some people from the mine Dad worked at had given it to her to give to her mom. Dad had fallen asleep a few nights ago, and he didn't wake up in the morning.

Nothing changed; her mother just kept starring at her. Lauren held back tears.

"Dad's gone to be with Lynne in Heaven, and you'll see them again when you get there," she said softly.

At the mention of Lynne's name, Lauren thought she saw a tear begin to form in her mom's eye. Lynne was born to her mom and dad exactly two years to the day after Lauren had been born. She never came home from the hospital; she died at three months of age. The family never talked about it. Death for some reason seemed to be off limits.

Doreen broke the silence and asked Lauren to get her a coffee so she could talk to her mom about the power of attorney. When Lauren returned to the room with the coffee, the power of attorney had been signed. Doreen claimed that all she did was help Lauren's mom hold the pen, but Lauren knew better. Doreen knew the mess the family would be in without those papers, so Lauren said nothing. Doreen had known her family for a long time, and had lived next door to them for fifteen years. Lauren babysat her children, which allowed her to make enough money to buy some new clothes for high school.

As they left the hospital, Doreen gave Lauren a hug and told her that she knew exactly the kind of children her parents had raised. She said she could trust any one of them with her life. Lauren and her siblings never mentioned their dad again in front of their mother. The Bible remained in her drawer beside her bed for the next ten years.

Lauren felt very confused over the next few weeks as she began cleaning out her parents' house. She needed all kinds of papers to fill out all the forms that were necessary when someone died. There seemed to be no semblance of order, and she had to fill out dozens of forms related to her dad's passing. Family and friends asked her if she needed any help, but she always refused the offers because of her pride and pain. She believed she was the only one who could do it and do it right.

She began to pull back and disconnect from the ones that cared about her. She was mad at the whole world, but especially at herself for being foolish enough to buy her father "the weapon" that he would use to kill himself.

She somehow managed to get herself to work, but she feared that someone would notice that things weren't right with her and that she

WHEN DID YOU HAVE YOUR LAST DRINK?

smelled like alcohol. She started testing her own blood at work and was surprised to discover that after her relatively short drinking career her liver function test results were slightly elevated. This scared her, because a few years prior to her fathers' death a cousin died of cirrhosis of the liver. He glowed yellow every time she'd go to see him to collect his blood. His liver was finished, and he died an alcoholic death at the age of forty-eight.

During those difficult times in her life, she felt like she was disconnecting from Matt. Because of the ongoing changes in her work schedule, she barely saw him. She got more done if she worked the afternoon shift, which gave her the morning to keep plugging away, cleaning out her parents' home. Matt got home from work at 6:00 p.m., but Lauren had already gone to work. When she got home at midnight, he was sleeping. When they finally got together there was alcohol between them. The drinking parties continued in their basement, and people continued to mark off the level of alcohol left in their bottle before they went home.

No one talked about her father's death. She and her siblings acted as though they were in denial and couldn't accept that he was dead. They all seemed to use the same tactics to avoid talking about what had happened that cold January morning outside their family home. That denial caused a lot of heartache, because they ended up arguing with each other whenever they were together. The real danger of the denial was that they could end up withdrawing and running away from each other.

Lauren realized that the denial they were all living with was probably fear based. If they openly talked about their pain, they'd be going against their parents' wishes. Children live what they learn at home, and their parents had taught them well. Don't talk about your pain. Stop crying, soldier on, and keep on marching.

One day Lauren told her brother, Karl, that their mom and dad hadn't always done what was best for the children. It was generational curse. Just because they put their pain under a bushel and never talked about it, didn't mean that their kids had to the same thing. Karl had a fit and yelled.

"You're telling me that Mom and Dad weren't good parents and raised us the wrong way? Well, I haven't got a clue what you're talking about, because they were the best parents a kid could ask for. You want me to bad mouth them just to make you happy. You need help, sis."

They never spoke about the issue again.

After their father's death, Lauren often asked her brothers about what took place that evening when they and their friends had been with their dad. Their answer was always the same: nothing happened. They'd left his place around 2:00 in the morning and headed out on their sleds. He seemed fine when they left him.

She also questioned why the police had been called and an investigation conducted. Her brothers explained that police investigations were always conducted when death occurred in the home. She never bothered to ask them how they felt about it all, because she knew they'd never answer that question. Their parents had taught them well … "mum's the word." The only thing they agreed upon after their father's death was to sell the house to Karl if he could come up with the money, and divide the small profit among his siblings.

Karl bought the house, and he and his family moved in the following month. Lauren was relieved to finish with all the paper work and put it behind her. She thought that she'd feel better and be able to move forward in her own life with Matt, but that never happened. She soon learned that all hope of becoming a mother was gone. After an ectopic pregnancy, the doctor told her that she'd never be able to conceive again.

This news devastated Lauren, so she started buying two bottles of brandy at a time. She went to a different liquor store every time she needed her drug of choice. She became more cautious, because it seemed like some of the clerks in the store were getting to know her, and that was very embarrassing. She grew more cautious at home, too. She hid two bottles of brandy instead of one, and never told Matt where she kept her stash. He'd started to enjoy a shot or two of brandy every day as well, and she wasn't willing to share her brandy with anyone—not even her husband.

The more she drank, the more she isolated herself. The only person she still trusted was her friend, Christina. A few months after Lauren's father's death, during lunch together, Christina told her about a man she knew who'd gone to a treatment center out of town for alcoholics and drug addicts. She said it was like a miracle had happened. The guy had been there for two months, and when he returned home he didn't look or act like the falling down drunk he used to be. He looked great; he'd stopped drinking, had gotten a job, and was constantly talking about his Higher Power, a Twelve Step program, and A.A.

Christina admitted that she really didn't know much about Twelve Step programs, but she'd heard about all the souls that had been saved by going to A.A. She then took a piece of paper out of her pocket with a phone number on it and handed it to Lauren.

"Here's the number of the treatment center," she said. "You never know … you may meet someone who needs it."

Lauren put the piece of paper into her jacket pocket. While driving home later, she started questioning her friend's reason for giving it to her. Did she think that she was drinking too much? And if so, why hadn't she just asked her instead of being sneaky about it?

When she arrived home she threw the paper into the garbage, because she'd convinced herself that Christina had an ulterior motive when she gave it to her. Who did she think she was to insinuate that Lauren drank too much?

The only explanation for what happened next was the will of God. Within an hour, Lauren found herself rummaging through the garbage, looking for that scrap of paper. By now she'd convinced herself that Christina meant no harm. Maybe one of her brothers drank too much and would come to her for help. She found the paper and put it in her kitchen cupboard in a container that held important numbers. She decided that it wasn't worth jeopardizing a friendship over a silly phone number.

Five months later, in a drunken stupor, Lauren found herself rummaging through her kitchen cupboards, looking for that little piece of paper Christina had given her. When she found it, she dialed the number.

"Hope Treatment Center," a friendly voice answered. "Can I help you?"

Lauren could hardly talk. "I need help," she whispered.

"We can help you," the voice said. "Let's talk. Is alcohol or drugs or both the reason you called us?"

"Yes," Lauren gingerly replied, "its' alcohol."

"When did you have your last drink?"

Lauren cleared her throat. "I'm having it right now"

It was 9:02 a.m., November 3, 1989.

It was no coincidence that the director of the treatment center just happened to answer the phone that dark and dreary day in November. After finding out that Lauren worked in a hospital, the director made an exception to the rule that a client needed to be sober for four weeks prior to being admitted to the program. Lauren didn't even have four hours of sobriety, yet the director asked her if she could get there the same day.

Years later, Lauren acknowledged that what took place that day had been prearranged by God. Ephesians 2:10 tells us that we are God's handiwork, created for a purpose. It was God's will that she go to that treatment center. It seemed to her that sometimes God remained anonymous by placing people in her life at exactly the moment she needed them the most. Many would call it coincidence, but Lauren believed that God has a sovereign plan for everyone. He gives us free will, but it's our job to rely on Him and follow His plan. He'll direct us if we accept direction and surrender our lives to Him.

10
WHAT ARE YOU DOING THERE?

When Lauren opened her bloodshot eyes and looked around, she didn't have the slightest idea where she was. It looked like a hospital room, but she didn't recognize anyone or anything. What had happened to her? Why was she in a bed in a strange place? And who was the woman sitting in a chair beside her bed?

"Hi Lauren," the woman said quietly. "Welcome back. I'm Mary. It looks like you had a good rest. Are you hungry or thirsty? Do you remember where you are?"

Lauren was about to say "no" when it all came back to her. The last thing she remembered was a kind but stern voice telling her to get a broom from the hall closet, sweep the stairwell, and then go sit in the chapel until they had a bed ready for her in detox.

Lauren cleared her throat and propped herself up on her elbows.

"Yes, I remember. I'm in an addiction center. Am I in detox? What day and time is it?" "It's November 4, and it's 7:00 p.m.," Mary replied.

"I must have been really tired; I think I lost a day somewhere."

All of the sudden Lauren started to panic and sat upright in the bed.

"Oh no … oh no … my husband doesn't know where I am, and my mother, my poor mother, she needs me. She's in hospital very sick. Can I use the phone?"

Mary assured her that she would let her use the phone to call her husband if she ate something and drank the protein drink that was sitting on the bedside table. Lauren agreed and was surprised to find out that she was hungry and that the food tasted good. Her head started to clear slightly by the time Mary gave her the phone.

She dialed her home number, and Matt answered on the second ring.

"Where are you? I was worried about you," he said. "You didn't even leave me a note like you usually do."

"I'm sorry," Lauren said. "I didn't mean to scare you. It seems that I'm in a detox ward, in an addiction center, in the small town of Murdock … not too far from where you and I went skiing with Jack."

"What are you doing there?" Matt asked.

Lauren looked at Mary who kept looking at her watch as if to say "hang up now!" Feeling rushed, Lauren quickly ended the conversation and hung up the phone.

In the days that followed, Lauren sensed the beginning of a slight disconnect between her and Matt. Was he emotionally starting to pull away from her? Was he embarrassed that his wife was in detox? Was he afraid that if Lauren quit drinking, he'd need to stop drinking too? Perhaps she was just imagining things and nothing had really changed between them.

Two days after the phone call, the doctor discharged Lauren from detox and told her that she was ready to start the twenty-eight day program. The staff gave her a tour of the facility and explained the house rules. They showed her the bedroom she'd share with another female client if and when one enrolled; for the time being, however, she'd be alone in the room. They left her in the client lounge and told her that within the next hour the other clients would join her and then they'd all go to an A.A. meeting that evening. A counselor would go with them, because it was being held in a church basement a mile away from their facility.

All Lauren could think about as she sat waiting were the house rules. She felt like she'd just enlisted in the army—no phone calls, no visitors, no writing letters, no leaving the property, no picture taking … and the list went on. There were more "can't do's" than "can do's," and by the time the other clients joined her, she'd convinced herself that she'd made a huge mistake. She didn't belong there; all she needed was a little undisturbed rest and some good food. She decided to leave the next morning and go back home. She didn't know how she was going to do that, because she didn't have her car. Christina had driven her there, and she didn't even have any money to take a bus. She was sure if she phoned Matt, though, he'd come and rescue her.

Her first A.A. meeting was dreadful; she felt so ashamed and was thankful that nobody knew who she was. She drank about ten cups of coffee and kept her head down the whole time while she listened to story after story about the terrible, shameful lives those so-called alcoholics lived. They all sounded like a bunch of losers to her, and she puffed up her pride by telling herself she was in far better shape than anyone sitting at the table. All that hugging and holding of hands and those stupid slogans were so childish.

She could hardly wait to get out of there, and when the meeting ended she dashed out of the building and started walking in the direction from which she had come. She was almost running by the time the counselor assigned to babysit her group caught up to her.

"So where do think you're going, young lady? You're not alone tonight, so you'll walk with me and your peers back to the center … understand? I make the rules, not you."

Lauren immediately fell into line with the other little soldiers and never said another word all the way back to the barracks. That counselor scared her. He looked and acted like an army sergeant. When she was safely in her room and the lights had been turned off, she lay on the bed and kept asking herself why she'd been so stupid. What was her problem? All she needed to do was drink less when she got back home. That would be easier than staying at the center.

Morning couldn't come soon enough. The loud voice announcing over the PA system that it was "time to rise and shine" threw Lauren back in time to a beautiful church camp she'd attended as a teenager. They also had a PA system with a speaker on the outside of the mess hall, and early in the morning the campers would hear "rise and shine … it's a beautiful day in the neighborhood." She could hardly wait for the day to begin, because it meant a new adventure. At the end of the day, she'd sit around a camp fire roasting marshmallows while listening to someone strumming on a guitar and singing. Everyone eventually joined in and they raised their voices towards the heavens singing "Kum Ba Yah, My Lord" and other favorites. The best part had been that there was boy there that Lauren fancied, and more often than not he'd take the seat beside her at the campfire.

She didn't feel like singing that morning; instead, she had felt like having a drink—a strong one. She thought about breaking the rules and using the phone to call Matt. Surely he'd rescue her. She'd tell him to pick up a bottle of her favorite brandy before he left the city.

Lauren went to the phone, but much to her dismay, a staff member caught her in the act and reprimanded her. He explained that two more strikes against her would result in her expulsion from the program. He said they'd have no problem kicking her out, because there was a long list of people who were serious about their recovery waiting to get in. If she wasn't serious about the gift that she'd been given, then she should run right back to where she'd come from.

"The world doesn't revolve around you, Lauren," he said as he walked away. "One day you'll understand."

This stopped Lauren in her tracks. At first she was confused, because she didn't know what he meant by that statement. Did he think she was arrogant and spoiled and full of selfish pride? He didn't know anything about how hard her life had been, so what gave him the right to talk down to her? It wouldn't be too much longer before she was "put into her place" again, and once again she would refuse to acknowledge that it might be her who had the problem … not the rest of the world.

Years later she found herself pondering a Bible verse that for some strange reason kept popping into her head. Was someone trying to tell her something? Matt constantly told her that she was stubborn and wanted things her own way. This aggravated her to no end, because she liked to think of herself as strong willed. Who did he think he was? The sergeant in the treatment center aggravated her without even using the word stubborn. He just insinuated it.

The words from Matthew 7:5 would come to haunt her until she couldn't stand it anymore. She was in such danger of drinking again that she not only went to more A.A. meetings, but she also found a good counselor at a family center and went to see her once a week. Eventually she came to acknowledge that she did have a log in her own eye.[1] Both Matt and the sergeant had figured her out. She was extremely disappointed to find out that when she got to the center of the universe, it wasn't about her. That knocked her off her pedestal, and she couldn't help but wonder who had put her there in the first place? She hadn't come into the world equipped with a pedestal to crawl up on.

By the grace of God, Lauren managed to stay in treatment for the full twenty-eight days and graduate from the program. For the first twelve days, she told herself daily that she'd leave the next day. It was on the thirteenth day when she was crying with her head down on the table that the stranger appeared with the "Pass it On/Proverb 3:5" card, and things began to change. Fifteen days later it was time to check out, and she didn't want to leave the safety of the center.

---

[1] Matthew 7:4-5

11

ACCEPTANCE, CHOICES, AND WISDOM

The most important things Lauren learned during her stay in treatment would carry her through life and provide her with a safe place to fall when her life fell apart. Matt came to visit her at the center, but when she saw him it felt like he was a stranger.

Lauren's counselor asked Matt to meet with her and Lauren so she could ask him a few questions. Lauren was nervous during the meeting, and she sensed that her husband felt the same way. They talked about what life had been like for them when they were both hiding behind liquor. Neither of them said very much, and when the counselor asked Matt why he'd stayed with Lauren, Matt responded with, "Because of the dog."

This comment embarrassed Lauren, because she believed Matt meant it. Matt never did like any kind of confrontation; he avoided all arguments like the plague and would escape reality by exiting the room, always with the dog in tow. Had they become parents, Lauren was sure Matt would have left the room with the children, too. He seemed to need to protect the dog from the trauma of listening to loud voices and yelling. Lauren once asked him why he always wanted to hide. He explained that he'd heard enough yelling when he was a kid, and he used to hide under the bed and worry about what was going to happen to him and his siblings if his parents kept it up.

After that meeting they didn't go to a counselor together again for twenty years … and even then they only went once in a sad attempt after his affair to talk about what had happened. Lauren thought she could win a prize for clamming up about her pain and fears, but Matt was even better at it than her. She was sure that if someone were holding a gun to his head insisting that he talk, he'd rather be shot than talk about his pain.

Before graduating from the program, Lauren celebrated her fortieth birthday in the center. Matt and Christina brought her gifts, and her peers gave her a mug with a lid that said: "You will always be surrounded by friends." She bought herself a little bell with a crucifix on the top of it from the gift store in the center, and for the first time in a very long time she felt needed and loved.

Amazing things happened to her during her stay. She learned how to hug people and to share her pain with them. After the "Pass it On/ Proverbs 3:5" card was given to her, she sensed such a feeling of gratitude for being the one chosen to receive that card. She was anxious to share her story with the world. Unknown to her at that time, the whole world didn't want to hear her story. In fact, even those closest to her didn't want to constantly hear about how wonderful the recovery programs and A.A. were.

She came to understand that the only place where she could talk openly about recovery and feel safe about it was with likeminded people. A.A. was based on the principle of sharing your story with other people who could relate, because they had the same malady as you did.

Alcoholics Anonymous began in 1935. Bill W., a stockbroker and a hopeless alcoholic under the spiritual guidance of the Oxford Groups in America, got sober and maintained that sobriety by working with other alcoholics. When Dr. Bob, a surgeon and a hopeless alcoholic, met Bill W., he found himself face to face with a fellow sufferer who had not only gotten sober but had learned how to maintain his sobriety. Soon Dr. Bob was also sober, and the spark that lit the flame of A.A. was born.

In 1939, Bill W. wrote the text that explained A.A's philosophy and methods. The core of it all is the Twelve Steps. Lauren was fascinated to learn that the Twelve Steps are closely linked to verses from the Bible. At first she found the Twelve Steps difficult to understand, but when she cross referenced them with Bible verses, she felt like she had a deeper understanding of what Bill W. had been talking about in 1939.

One of the most empowering moments for her occurred when she accepted the fact that she needed to willingly participate in the group counseling sessions, and that she wasn't as smart as she thought she was. During one session, a counselor asked Lauren how long her father had been dead. When Lauren responded with ten months, the counselor acted surprised.

"That's not very long ago, Lauren," he said. "I thought you were talking about years since he passed. It takes a long time to heal from the death of a parent. I want you to remember when you leave here that you weren't the one who picked up the glass of rum and poured it down your father's throat. He made that choice. You don't own that one; he owns it. Dead or not, it still belongs to him—not you. Alcoholics prefer their drug of choice, but when they don't have it, they'll drink anything with alcohol in it. Your father would have found something else to drink if you hadn't brought him that rum."

By validating her pain, the counselor gave Lauren a place to start grieving the death of her father. He also gave her permission to forgive herself for the role she thought she'd played in his death. When we don't forgive ourselves or others, we live in a constant state of suppressed anger and fear, and we prevent ourselves from growing in our faith. Tragically, we waste our lives looking for that "almighty high" in people, places, and things.

Lauren felt like her brain was a sponge. The more she learned, the more she wanted to learn. She realized that she never even considered the fact that alcoholism might be a disease. She'd always been under the impression that alcoholics were just a bunch of weak willed people who didn't have a home or family to go to.

She received a real eye opener when she went to a lecture given by a doctor who was board certified in addiction. He explained that the jury is still out concerning alcoholism. Some believe it's a matter of nature, based on a genetic predisposition, and others believe it stems more from nurturing and the way you were brought up or the life experiences you had.

As a disease, alcoholism is perhaps the only disease in which the affected person holds the key to recovery. Alcoholics who go to a treatment center because they want to get better have to do the work. Doctors can't automatically cure this disease like they can some others. That doctor also talked about "cold-turkey" abstinence. When someone is "on the wagon," they're not drinking. It doesn't mean that they're in recovery; it simply means that they aren't drinking. The problem with this approach is that unless an alcoholic is on the wagon with other alcoholics and holding A.A. meetings, praying, and talking about their drinking problems, nothing changes. These people dedicate their life to taking a free ride on a wagon, but don't contribute in any way to keep the wagon running well. They're simply too lazy to do the work, or they don't care enough about themselves or their families to work towards living a life free from guilt, shame, and unforgiveness.

Usually permanent wagon riders are not much fun, make poor life choices, and end up in worse shape than when they were drinking all the time. The only difference is that now they don't have a bottle or a glass in their hand; however, they still think like a practicing alcoholic. It's called "stinking thinking," and their behavior matches it.

The doctor also stressed that alcoholism is a family disease. Everyone needs help—not just the drinker. In order to save themselves from the alcoholic's blame and shame game, family members need to seek outside help before the alcoholic destroys their lives as well. Help can be found through Al-Anon groups and family or spiritual counseling. Family members should never cover up for the alcoholic. A child should not be expected to act like an adult because the parent is too drunk to do their job. Children from alcoholic homes often suffer emotional, spiritual, and physical damage. Without intervention, they may grow up constantly looking for approval and not knowing what a normal family looks like. They have trouble with trust and intimacy in relationships and judge themselves without mercy. They live with an "everything must be my fault" kind of attitude or a mindset that says, "You're not enough; you must do better."

Lauren felt like she was just beginning learn and understand how the program worked when the time came for her to go home. She was petrified, so she went to the chapel before leaving to pray and give thanks to God for giving her a second chance.

In the year that followed her discharge from the center, she returned to weekend retreats to learn more. It continued to feel like home and would always hold a special place in her heart. It was almost like she'd been preparing herself for what was to come. The days following her return to her home town and her job were difficult; however, she didn't drink during those stressful times, and there was no doubt in her mind that if it hadn't been for God's mercy and grace, she'd either be dead or writing her story from a jail cell.

12

IS THERE ANYTHING TO READ
ON THIS TUG BOAT?

Matt took a day off work, and he and their dog drove to Murdock to pick Lauren up once she'd completed the program. He arrived just in time for the graduation ceremony. Each client who'd completed the twenty-eight day program received a pin with a picture of an acorn on it to symbolize that small acorns can grow into big oak trees. They also received a card with the words "You don't need to die for a drink" on the front and the Serenity Prayer on the back.

The director of the center reminded the clients of what was expected of them when they got home. If Lauren were to summarize what the director said, it would read: "Go to meetings ... get a sponsor ... be active in your recovery ... pay your story forward ... pray really hard but work even harder ... pretend that there's a big video camera in the heavens recording every move you make and every word you say ... hold yourself accountable for what you do ... apologize quickly and when necessary make amends .... love your neighbor as yourself and be kind to everyone, even the poor and the unfortunate ... don't live with unforgiveness in your heart ... it will destroy you and everyone around you ... ask God to help you to learn how to forgive ... and practice gratitude every day."

Everyone hugged and made a promise to keep in touch. Then it was over. Lauren didn't say much on the way home, because she was at a loss for words. She had gotten used to the lingo of the treatment center, and she really didn't know what to say to Matt. He was still a practicing alcoholic, and she feared that she'd sound like she expected him to go into treatment too.

Upon arriving home, before she even took her coat off, Lauren went to the cupboard that housed her hidden bottle of brandy. It was still there, so she poured the contents down the drain, making sure Matt didn't see her. She was sure he would say something, because brandy was expensive and he wouldn't be too happy to see it going down the drain. Next she went downstairs to check out how much liquor was at the bar. Bottles with black lines on the labels lined the shelves, and the refrigerator was full of beer. Nothing had changed in her absence. The room stunk like a tavern bar, so she found the air freshener spray and sprayed the whole room. Despite the freezing weather, she opened a large window facing the lake and breathed in the cold fresh air.

Once upstairs she unpacked her bags and placed the bell with the crucifix on her kitchen window sill. She hoped that every time she looked at it she'd be reminded not to drink. After Matt left her, she would sleep with that bell/crucifix in her hand. When she'd awaken she'd see its imprint on her hand. She must have been hanging onto it very tightly during the night.

The next six months went by quickly. Lauren feared going back to work in case her co-workers knew where she'd disappeared to. The only person from work who knew about the center was her friend, Bruce, and his wife, Marion. She'd trusted them enough to tell them where she was. Bruce had written to her while she was in treatment, and he'd encouraged her to stick it out and finish the program. In the end, returning to work wasn't as difficult as she'd anticipated. Everyone welcomed her back and asked no questions.

Lauren joined an A.A. group and attended meetings every Tuesday at 7:00 p.m. Even on the darkest of days, when she had to force herself to go to a meeting, it was worth the effort. She always came out of the meeting feeling better than when she went in. Fellowship with likeminded people was always rewarding, because everyone was in the same boat trying to do the same thing—stay sober.

Matt continued to drink, but things were different. When a bottle was emptied at the bar in their basement, it wasn't replaced, because the owner of that bottle stopped coming to their home. Word spread quickly throughout the drinking community that Lauren wasn't drinking any more. Lauren took no offense at the change in their friends' behaviour. She understood that she was a threat to them because she was different. One sober person talking about recovery at a table with a bunch of serious drinkers doesn't make for a comfortable conversation. Unless you're ready to do something about your problem you don't want to take the chance of talking to an ex-drinker, because you may have to look at yourself in order to measure up.

A month after Lauren returned home, she and Matt spent a weekend at a beautiful lodge in prime boating country—a wedding gift from Christina. All they had to do was book the weekend of their choice. They hadn't used it the summer of their wedding because there had been too much going on. Instead, they decided to go the May long weekend the following spring.

They contacted friends of Christina's, who both of them had met before, to invite them to stop by and see them at the lodge. In return, the friends invited Matt and Lauren to join them on their prized tug boat for a tour of the islands.

On the day Matt and Lauren left for what they hoped would be a great weekend, Lauren had been sober for 170 days, and Matt for zero days. Lauren was concerned about being the only non-drinker in the group. While in treatment, she'd been told that it wasn't a good idea to be boxed in with people who drank. If she had an escape route planned beforehand, and knew she could get out if she was tempted to drink, then depending on who she was with, it might be okay, but she shouldn't make a habit of it. The center advised her to make new friends and stay away from the drinkers.

When they reached the lodge, they spotted a large tug boat moored to the dock. It looked out of place surrounded by the majestic power boats. As they were heading towards the dock, they heard their names being called. Sure enough, it was Bill and Sally and two friends of theirs whom Lauren and Matt had never met. Introductions were made, the skipper roared "all aboard," and Lauren jumped in.

"Just give a minute," Matt said. "I've got a cooler of ale in the car. I'll be right back."

It was 11:00 a.m. on a beautiful calm day when they headed out of the channel into bigger water. Lauren calculated that they were going about three miles an hour, and it felt like they were getting nowhere. Everyone with the exception of Lauren had a drink in their hand and seemed to be enjoying themselves. When she couldn't listen to another word about what a beautiful tug it was and what an awesome job had been done to restore the old gal, Lauren set up a lawn chair in the back of the boat and asked Sally if there were any books that she could read. Sandy handed her a bunch of paperback novels, and Lauren thanked her.

Great, she thought. *I can at least read until they dock this monster snail.*

Unfortunately, the novels were all *Harlequin Romances.* It would be the first and last time Lauren would read one of those sappy books. It was either that or jump off the boat and swim to shore (which she considered doing).

Around 3:30 p.m. the skipper suggested that if they wanted to make it back to the liquor store before it closed, they should turn the old gal around and head back to the docks. Lauren sighed with relief and prayed that the boat had a speed higher than just "putt … putt."

By 5:30 p.m., everyone except Lauren was getting a little antsy, because the docks were still a long way off for a tug boat. The liquor store closed at 6:00 p.m. and wouldn't open until the following Tuesday because of the long weekend.

As luck would have it for the drinkers aboard, the tug pulled into the docks at 5:52. Lauren wasn't even out of the lawn chair by the time the girls put the fenders down and the guys tied the bow and stern lines. Everyone booted it to the liquor store, which was a trailer parked only minutes away from the docks.

Lauren would always remember watching Matt come out of the liquor store with two cases of beer, and wondering why he would need forty-eight more bottles when he already had a case in the car and a spare at home. That was ninety-six bottles of beer for a long weekend! When she took a minute to think about it, she had to admit that she knew the answer. Long weekends and holidays play havoc with serious drinkers.

The fear of "what if" is very real. What if I run out and can't get any more of my drug because the liquor store is closed? It's risky business if you happen run out.

"Hey, let's get going," Matt yelled at Lauren. "They're all coming to our room for a few drinks. This beer is heavy. I'm heading for room #313."

"Okay," Lauren yelled back. "I'm just going for a walk through the town. I'll be back soon."

Lauren took off like she was in a marathon. She kept running and running in search of some quiet place to sit down and think. The town was small, and she couldn't even go for a coffee because she had no money with her. She still had on her shorts and t-shirt, and the air was starting to cool down. She felt a chill when she stopped to catch her breath.

She'd run right past a small, quaint church, and without knowing why, she suddenly turned around and headed back in the direction of the church. She hoped that the church door might be unlocked so that she could go in and sit for a moment.

She walked down the path leading to the front door and turned around to see if anyone was watching her before she tried the handle and the door opened. Inside the quaint little church were twelve rows of pews on both sides facing the altar. She felt a reverence there unlike anything she'd ever experienced. She'd been inside many churches, some of them when she was on vacation in Europe, but this church was different. Beautiful spring flowers adorned the altar, and through a window facing west you could see the sun setting over the bay.

She sat down close to the back of the church and stared at the crucifix on the altar. She caught herself whispering, as though she wasn't the only one in the church.

"Help me ... please help me. I'm not going to make it. I'm so afraid I'll drink again. Please ... please direct my path ... make me strong and courageous enough to keep moving in the right direction. Amen."

She wasn't sure how long she sat there, but it was dark by the time she left and found her way back to room #313. There she discovered Matt passed out on the bed, the partiers gone, and beer bottles everywhere.

She washed her face, brushed her teeth, and crawled into the bed beside Matt. She listened to him snoring, and then finally dozed off by repeating the Serenity Prayer over and over again in her head.

The next morning Matt opened his eyes and announced: "I'm never going to drink again." As far as Lauren knew, he never did.

13

YOU CAN'T WISH FOR THE
THINGS YOU CAN'T CHANGE

Matt followed through with the pledge to never drink again, but now he and Lauren were often at a loss for what to do. So much of their time had been devoted to drinking, and without alcohol in their lives, nothing exciting ever happened. Life seemed to be moving in a straight line with no highs or lows. There were no more surprise visitors stopping by for a quick drink, no more laughter at the bar, no hiding liquor, and no more heated arguments fueled by alcohol. It was almost like they had leprosy and were doomed to face long lasting mental issues and social stigma.

If Lauren could have removed the bar in the basement she would have, because it was no longer being used. She liked getting rid of the old and bringing in the new. When she decided that it was time for all the bar paraphernalia to go, she was surprised to find so much stuff. There were bottle openers, coasters, shot glasses, mugs, brandy snifters, wine glasses, ice buckets, a picture of the wedding party holding those stupid beer mugs, and every size of glass imaginable to serve liquor in. The only thing left on the bar was her antique bubble gum machine.

She drove to the city dump and, one by one, threw the "drinking bags" into the dumpster. She tried to hit the side of the metal dumpster so that she could hear the sound of glass shattering. After each bag she threw in she yelled, "Yahoo!" Before leaving the dump, she raised her head towards the heavens and said "thank you."

She would make more trips to the same dump in the years to come. Sometimes she would have tears in her eyes as the bags were thrown into the dumpster, and sometimes she would tell herself what a fool she'd been to waste so much money. Everything in those garbage bags had cost her something ... only to end up in a dumpster.

Years later, after numerous sessions with her counselor, Lauren found herself accepting and validating the fact that she and Matt had emotionally started to detach the day she admitted herself into the Hope Treatment Center. It had changed their relationship because she had changed. Perhaps Matt was afraid that if he didn't quit drinking, they wouldn't make it as a couple.

Although they had a "no drinking rule" in common, they had different ideas about what recovery meant and how to stay sober. Lauren adamantly believed that going cold turkey would never work for her. Her strong will didn't bend easily, and she'd fight to her death to prove she was right. Someone, or something, had to bring her to her knees and break her. She compared herself to a horse that had never been broken. She needed to be trained in the same way a horse trainer would break in a horse, with constant reminders that she wasn't going to get away with just following her instincts.

When we lose something, either willingly or unwillingly, we need to replace it with something else. You can't just take the bottle away from the baby and expect the baby to jump up and make himself lunch. We need to learn a new way to act and think and behave. As children age, they learn how to make lunch for themselves, and then how to go out and get a job to make money so that they can buy the food to make their own lunch.

In the treatment center, Lauren learned that she needed to find something to replace drinking, and not to just "jump on a wagon" and hope for the best. She needed God to direct her to people that could help her. She'd been given a book of instructions on how to live without alcohol. If she hadn't been willing to participate in her recovery, nothing would have changed. She thought of it as going back to school to learn how to live differently, and she knew it would take work and a willingness to unlearn old behaviors. Unfortunately, her ego kept getting in the way and slowed down the process. She realized that there was no quick fix in recovery, and there never would be. It was a "one day at a time" program that required her to take down the walls of defense and be active in her recovery for the rest of her life.

Matt ended his drinking by sheer will power—a brave and remarkable thing to do. Often Lauren told him that she hoped he'd quit drinking for himself and not just for her. Matt met her questions about his past drinking with questions of his own, and he wanted to know why she kept talking about the past. She explained that while in treatment she learned that the key to recovery lies within. It's not an external quick fix you can find in a gym. Going to a gym might make your outsides look better, but the heart of your problems remains untouched. The answers were always found in our past and in our willingness to walk through that pain and not run away from it.

Even during the darkest days of Matt's life, when he would have qualified for a month in rehab, he was unwilling to go. He made it clear to Lauren that he'd never go to A.A. either, which only required a willingness to quit drinking from its members. She cut him some slack, because she believed either he was afraid to talk about his past because it was too painful, or he'd been raised in a home like hers that had a poster on the wall that said: "Stop crying or I'll give you something to cry about."

An old Chinese Proverb teaches: "Give a man a fish and you feed him for a day. Teach a man to fish and you feed him for a lifetime." Lauren understood that no matter what she said or did, or what kind of example she set, Matt didn't want to learn how to fish; he acted like he was satisfied with someone giving him a fish every day.

14

OH WHAT A TANGLED WEB WE WEAVE

L auren learned that it wasn't her responsibility to fix her husband and that her way wasn't the only way. That didn't change the fact that she desperately wanted Matt to walk the road of recovery with her. Both of them had a lot of potential to become the best they could be. Her dream was to pay their story forward and give couples hope that no matter what had taken place in their marriage, it didn't have to end in divorce.

Lauren's dream was shattered when it became obvious that Matt didn't want to become the best he could be with her by his side. His behavior towards her indicated that he was envisioning a new life with the "other woman," Jessica, by his side.

Lauren believed Jessica was putting pressure on him, like in most affairs, to leave his wife and move in with her. By the time Matt finally broke his code of silence, Jessica had found another man. In the years that followed, people asked Lauren why Matt hadn't fought to win Jessica back. She always answered by saying that she didn't know, and they would have to ask him. She felt like he'd put himself into a witness protection program and disappeared off the face of the earth. Secretly, she suspected that he ran away to grieve the loss of his girlfriend and was beating himself up for not leaving his wife sooner. Knowing Matt as well as she did, there was no doubt in her mind that he blamed himself for the loss of the relationship.

A few years after Matt quit drinking, Lauren suggested that he see a counselor to help him work through why it was so difficult for him to make decisions. As usual, he ignored her. The phrase, "I shouldn't have" graced his vocabulary often. She begged him to start believing in himself and the choices that he made. From the day she met him to the day he left her, drinking or not drinking, he managed to get at least one "I shouldn't have" in every day. She wondered if it was his way of reminding himself that he wasn't capable of making good choices. It was painful for Lauren to watch him, because he constantly talked about what he shouldn't have done, instead of what he did do. That kind of thinking is detrimental, because it fixates on the past and leaves no room for gratitude or forgiveness.

Lauren often left the room because she couldn't stand hearing him chastise himself for what he thought was a wrong choice. Where had that originated? He hadn't come into the world saying "I shouldn't have been born." She never told Matt that she suspected "I'm not enough" went hand and hand with "I shouldn't have," and that the fear of making the wrong decision caused him to "fence sit." She knew he would just exit the room before she finished the sentence, and under his breath mutter, "You don't know what you're talking about."

It was rather pompous of Lauren to think that she had Matt figured out. She was the first one to admit that she had a very vivid imagination and that her feelings often lied; however, her theory was based on much more than her feelings.

During the time Matt was dating Jessica, he talked about her constantly. Lauren had no clue what was going on between them. She couldn't figure out why she'd get sick to her stomach every time Matt mentioned Jessica. One day it would be, "She's very beautiful," and the next day it was, "Her counselor told her to leave her husband." He also told Lauren that Jessica had a dance pole in her bedroom, and that her father had told her she was stupid. He also felt bad that Jessica had to plan her own birthday party.

Every word Matt said about Jessica made Lauren feel nauseous, and she had no idea why. Sometimes she had to run to the washroom to vomit. One day Matt came home from a ski trip with a t-shirt and a wooden carving of an owl. He told Lauren to pick one gift for herself, and the other one would go to Jessica. Lauren questioned why he would bring Jessica a gift.

"Because when she goes somewhere," he explained, "she brings me a gift."

Lauren ran to the washroom and vomited, returning a few moments later.

"I'm not feeling so great today," she said. "Must be a flu bug. About the gifts … I'll take the owl. The t-shirt looks a little small for me, and you know I don't like anything tight."

On another occasion, Matt came home from work quite livid. Lauren asked him what was wrong.

"Jessica doesn't need me to pick her up anymore on my way to work," he said. "I'm going to be out $5.00 a day for gas money."

"Does she have her own car now?" Lauren asked.

"No," he fired back. "She told me today that she's going out with some guy she calls her new boyfriend, and he's picking her up. I've seen him with her, and he's a big b_____!"

Before he finished his sentence, Lauren was in the washroom vomiting again.

Lauren knew that her feelings sometimes lied to her, but she soon learned that her gut always spoke the truth. Some researchers call the gut the "intelligence of the unconscious," or the "second brain." For decades they've known about the connection between the brain and the gut.

15

NEVER DENY OR IGNORE
THE WARNINGS

After nine years of marriage, Lauren and Matt sold their home and bought another home a few miles away on a smaller body of water and off the beaten path. They rarely had visitors. Word spread quickly that Matt had quit drinking, too. It felt as though they'd put a sign on the mailbox at the road that said: "No Drinkers Allowed."

They isolated themselves and made little effort to cultivate new friendships. Ironically, they had everything going for them, but neither of them acted like it. Lauren worked steady afternoon shifts, and Matt worked steady day shifts. Their schedules didn't allow for much time to be together. Lauren had friends at work and through A.A., and Matt had golfing and skiing buddies. Lauren was close to her family and went to see her mother at the hospital often. Nothing had changed with her mom; she remained silent and never spoke a word right up to the end. It was difficult to watch her suffer. Matt never visited Lauren's mother in hospital, and rarely saw his own family. Even at Christmas he didn't celebrate with family, but instead went by himself to visit the parents of a friend.

By the time a realtor pounded the For Sale sign into the ground next to the mailbox, Matt was no longer living in that house, and his name had been removed from the deed. Lauren was the sole owner, and before it was sold, she had a lot of time to think about what had taken place in that house. With any kind of luck, maybe she could dig up a few good memories to take with her.

She vividly remembered the day she and Matt had taken ownership of the house. She was putting the key into the lock to open the front door, and a snake fell on her shoulder. She brushed it off, but not knowing where it had come from and envisioning a house full of snakes, she'd refused to go in.

She didn't know when Matt would be home, so she called a "critter catcher" and asked him to get there as fast as he could. While waiting for him to arrive, she thought about Eve and the serpent in the Garden of Eden. When she was a child, her dad had told her all about the talking snake that had tempted Eve to take a bite of the forbidden fruit. She'd gone against God's wishes when she bit into that apple.

Her dad never did tell her where Adam was when that had happened. Was he with Eve, or was he off exploring the garden and she had to track him down? If Adam had been there, you'd think he would have convinced Eve to run in the opposite direction. God had warned them about that one tree. It was as though He'd put red flags all around the tree, and Eve had ignored them all.

On that day in the garden, not only did Eve question God's words and warnings, but she also bought into the serpent's lies when she ate the fruit. That one act resulted in her spiritual death, and the consequences destroyed her entire family's future—a huge price to pay for an act of disobedience.

When the "serpent" had fallen on Lauren, Matt had been on the golf course. He should have been there to celebrate the opening of their new home. She needed him to be there, but he had insisted that she get the keys and open up the house on her own, promising to be there as soon as he could.

Fortunately, Lauren acted quickly after she brushed the snake off her shoulder. She grabbed a pail that her cleaning supplies were in and turned it upside down over the snake. The "critter catcher" had told her that he was happy she'd acted quickly and trapped it. He told her that it was a very rare breed of snake and not common to their area. After checking the house over from top to bottom, he gave her an all clear. He figured that a bird had been flying over at the exact moment Lauren turned the front door knob, and had dropped its prey on her shoulder. He asked Lauren if he could have the snake, and she had been more than happy to pay him and give him the snake as a tip.

Lauren never bought his story, because three months later a snake crawled into her kitchen when she opened that same door. She trapped the snake under a garbage can and called a neighbor to come over and remove it from her kitchen. There seemed to be snakes everywhere on that property. Even on the cedar dock at the water's edge she would often see a large water snake sunning itself.

Lauren spent a lot of time looking down while she lived in that house. She remained on guard just in case another snake tried to slither into her home. Maybe if she'd spent more time looking up, she would have been better prepared to handle the curve balls that life would soon throw her way.

Throughout the Scriptures, the serpent generally represents the devil. It was in the form of a snake that the devil first manifested himself to the human race. Some theologians believe that Satan's work of deception began in the Garden of Eden and has continued worldwide ever since. The only way to escape Satan's deceptions is by simple and pure devotion to Christ, demonstrated by obeying His Word by His Spirit.

In time, Lauren would come to believe that Satan the serpent had played a role in both of her marriages. Her first marriage, which ended in divorce after seven years, had a few snake stories, too. Her cats would often come into the house carrying a trophy snake, and when they would drop it to show her, the snake would sometimes slither away and cause her lots of concern.

After Matt moved out of the house, a woman whose husband worked with him visited Lauren. She insinuated that Matt had had more than one affair and that the most recent one probably wouldn't be his last. Lauren was so embarrassed and hurt that she couldn't face anybody; she just wanted to hide from the world. Friends of hers offered her their camp, and she took them up on the offer. She wanted to be completely alone, so she chose to sleep in the change room in the steam bath at the water's edge. Other than her dog, she thought she was completely alone. In the mornings, the water in the steam room was still warm, so she washed up in there.

On the morning of her seventh day there, she went into the steam room only to be met by the biggest snake she'd ever seen. It was curled up on the still-warm rocks on the stove and didn't look like it was going anywhere. Within ten minutes she packed everything and she and her dog were in the truck, leaving a trail of dust behind them.

On the way home all she could think about was that snake. She felt like she'd been close to sleeping with the enemy. All that had been between them was a thin cedar wall. As the years rolled by, Lauren wondered if she'd been close to sleeping with the enemy in both her marriages. What more could she have done to keep the enemy at bay? If she'd had her full armor of God on, would she have been able to stand firm against the schemes of the devil, just like Paul said in Ephesians 6:13? In the wake of Matt's infidelity, Lauren's willingness to accept all the blame for her failed marriages disturbed her the most. Where had that come from? Did she not have any boundaries in her life? Did she not know who owned what? She was no saint, but she wasn't the one who'd had an affair. Why was she so hard on herself? The answer would soon be revealed to her at a counseling session. It would be a watershed moment, and all she could say was, "You've got to be kidding me!"

After Matt's affair, Lauren felt like she was back in school, only this time she was in school to learn as much as she could about Satan. She read and contemplated every Bible verse she could find, and she asked lots of questions about Lucifer, the fallen angel. She concluded that Satan liked to ruin marriages. All he needed was one person in the family who wasn't wearing any spiritual armor and could be easily tempted to leave a door open so he could slither in. He lays in wait, looking for a crack in the relationship and an opportune moment, and then he strikes. He's very fond of adulterous relationships, because they not only take down the adulterer, but everyone in their family, too. Everybody suffers because of the selfish act of disobedience of two people.

Sexual immorality results in a rage and anger that cause horrific things to happen. Spouses kill each other in a fit of rage, or commit suicide. Jails are full of suffering people who took the law into their own hands. People go bankrupt trying to support two or more families. Lawyers get richer because court battles over infidelity can go on indefinitely with no resolution in sight. Children, even the adult ones, suffer and feel divided because they don't know which side to take. Children grow up to be what they learned at home, so children from divorced families have a much higher divorce rate.

Lauren soon came to believe that even the worst things that had ever happened to her were not without purpose, but had laid the ground work for a new life. She was able to transform from a victim into a victor, in the same way that a caterpillar morphs into a butterfly. All she had to do was trust God with all her heart and not to lean on her own understanding. He would teach her, if she asked in His name, how to forgive her adulterous husbands, and anyone else who had wounded her. It was a big order, but she was up to it, because with God in her life, all things were possible. After all, He was the one who made us in His image. He didn't design us to be victims and live miserable lives; He designed us to overcome and live victorious with joy and hope in our hearts as we wait for Him to call us home to our eternal resting place.

16

IN SICKNESS
AND IN HEALTH

It had been a horrific and terrifying year. Something was wrong with Matt. Lauren went into action, trying to figure out why he'd been acting so strangely. He looked terrible and wasn't sleeping, and he could barely look at her. Lauren, fearing the worst, called a doctor she knew and asked him to order blood work on Matt, because she was scared that he was suffering from some kind of ailment that would kill him. His mental health also concerned her, because he kept talking about being afraid that he would end up like their niece, who'd been diagnosed with schizophrenia.

Lauren kept encouraging Matt to talk to the health nurse where he worked in the hopes that maybe through the Employee Assistance Program he could get some help. Eventually he did go to see the nurse, but when Lauren asked him about it, he said that she was no help at all. The only thing the nurse said to him was, "Good luck with your future endeavors."

Lauren couldn't believe that anyone in that position would say such a thing. What was wrong with her? Couldn't she see that there was something wrong with him? In the years that followed, Lauren would come to understand why no help had been offered to him. Jessica worked in the same place as Matt, and it became obvious to Lauren that the health nurse—and probably everyone that worked there—knew about his affair with Jessica. Obviously the nurse didn't have any tricks up her sleeve to help a guy who was being unfaithful to his wife.

The stranger Matt acted, the harder Lauren worked to try to find a way to help him. She was happy the day Matt told her that he'd made an appointment with a counselor. When she asked him if he knew anything about the person who was going to counsel him, he told her that Jessica had gone to him, and she liked him. When Lauren questioned him about the man's qualifications, Matt said that the counselor had told Jess to leave her husband, and she did. He added that she said she'd never been happier. When Lauren had asked him if he thought counselors were supposed to tell their clients what to do, he responded with, "That's what those guys get paid to do."

Within two weeks of that conversation, Matt told Lauren that he was going to a fortune teller, and he was going to get a tattoo.

"Did you just pull the names of a fortune teller and a tattoo artist out of the phone book?" Lauren asked.

"No," he replied. "Jess had been to both of them and said they were good."

The insanity continued, putting Lauren under stress and endangering her health. She felt like she was being emotionally tortured and didn't know by whom or why.

Five years prior to that time, she'd been very sick. She felt like she'd picked up a terrible flu bug and was struggling to do the simplest of chores. She couldn't go to work because she was having trouble thinking and walking, as though her whole body was in the process of shutting down. Every muscle in her body ached, and she suffered from extreme fatigue.

It took eight months and a referral to an out of town specialist before she got a diagnosis of Fibromyalgia, often referred to as FMS—a disorder characterized by widespread musculoskeletal pain accompanied by fatigue, sleep, memory, and mood issues. Researchers believe that FMS amplifies painful sensations by affecting the way your brain processes pain signals. Researchers also believe that it may be the result of a physical or emotional trauma and is somehow connected to the central nervous system.

The most difficult part of FMS is dealing with the shame and guilt that accompanies it. You still look the same to the outside world, but inside you feel like you're dying. If you break your leg and have trouble walking around, most people sympathize with you because they can see that you're struggling. FMS is not visible to the eye; you can't see it, and many people aren't even aware that such a disorder exists. Consequently, people have difficulty sympathizing with sufferers because they look perfectly normal to them. People with FMS often feel like nobody understands how they feel. When their pain isn't validated by doctors or family, FMS patients can feel like they're just crazy, and that their pain isn't real. Some people accuse them of faking it just to get attention, or they tell them that they need to see a physiatrist.

The doctor who finally diagnosed Lauren told her to reduce the stress in her life and try not to be too sedentary. He suggested walking a short distance every day and stopping when she got tired. He also told her that she'd never return to work, especially since she was only one year short of being retired.

Lauren was grateful to get a diagnosis, but not happy to hear that there was no magic pill to take her pain away. In time, she tried to do the same thing she'd done when she quit drinking— just take one day at a time. Do the best you can to accept whatever illness or disorder you have, and then acknowledge that it's your pain and don't make other people pay for what belongs to you. Be courageous and active in your recovery, and try to walk one step further every day. Pray to God for the wisdom to know and understand that even on your darkest and most painful days, He is with you, and when you can't walk, He'll carry you.

Matt stayed with Lauren during this time; however, he wasn't emotionally available to her. He seemed to be mad all the time, which she read as frustration at his own inability to make her better. He may also have been afraid that she wouldn't get better, and it had come across as anger. What they did have in common was shared anger at the hospital where Lauren worked, because they refused to give her the money owing to her. They didn't like or trust the diagnosis she'd been given. It took a year and a lawyer before she got access to her pension—a plan she'd paid into for thirty years.

Lauren tried to follow the doctor's orders, but Matt's behavior caused her so much stress she felt like she was moving backwards and had lost all her coping skills. The real problem was that she didn't know what she was trying to cope with. She felt like she was fighting an invisible demon in the fog, worried that it was going to kill her. The more bizarre his behavior became, the more Lauren suffered.

In December the Christmas cards started arriving. One card was made out to "Mr. and Mrs." with no return address on it. Upon opening it, Lauren was sure that a mistake had been made and the card wasn't intended for them. It wished them a Merry Christmas and was signed "Jessica, Mark, and Robin." Matt snatched the card out of Lauren's hands and threw it down on the table.

"Wow," he roared. "That didn't take long!"

She asked him again who the people were.

"That's Jessica," he replied. "She's the woman who traveled to work with me. It looks likes she's gotten herself a whole new family. The guy she's with must have a kid."

"Didn't you tell me just a few weeks ago that she was single and had won a trip to Cuba?" Lauren asked.

"Yeah I did," Matt replied. "From what I hear, Jess and the big "B" plan to go together."

As Lauren left the room, her gut yelled at her, "Danger! Danger!"

Just a few weeks earlier, Matt had rushed in from work and, without saying a word, ran to the computer. When she went to see him and ask what the big rush was all about, he'd told her that he was entering a contest to win a trip to Cuba. She asked him who he'd take with him if he won, and he replied that he didn't know. That really hurt her.

As a result of those danger feelings, Lauren devised a new tactic to try to get Matt to talk about what was bothering him. Every couple of days for the next two months she asked him the same three questions. Before asking, she told him that if he had anything to talk about, she'd listen and they'd resolve it together, no matter what the issue was.

The three questions she asked were: Did you rob a bank? Did you murder someone? Did you have an affair? His answers were always the same. Without hesitation he would say, "No, no, and no."

By the beginning of March, nothing had changed, and Lauren felt extremely fatigued and desperate. She stopped asking Matt the questions and decided that if she wanted to survive, she had to get out of there. She didn't know where she would go or what she would do, but she packed a small bag so she'd be ready when the day came to leave.

On March 7 of that year, she approached Matt and told him about her plans to leave. She hoped that he would stop her, but he didn't.

"Okay," he said as he picked up his gym bag and walked out the door.

Lauren grabbed her packed bag and the dog, jumped into her truck, and drove down the long driveway, stopping at the mailbox. She looked to the left and the right, and then said out loud, "Lord, I don't have a clue where to go or what to do. Please direct my path. Amen." With that, she made a sharp left and headed to the gas station. By the time she filled up her truck, she had an inkling of what direction she should be going, and she never looked back until she got there. She'd arrived at the place that had a piece of her heart.

17

I NEED ANSWERS
OR I WILL SURELY DIE

Lauren arrived in Murdock, the home of the treatment center where she'd been a client seventeen years before. She drove to the center, parked, and sat in her truck, staring at the building. Behind those doors a miracle had happened. She was still sober and extremely grateful that she was. She had been consumed and controlled by fear when she was admitted, and she was still consumed by fear when she was discharged, except now the fear didn't control her every move. She'd left the center carrying a manual on how to stay sober, a bell with a crucifix, and a card that said "Pass it On/Proverbs 3:5."

Fortunately, she'd met many people who guided her in the right direction. After both betrayals, she sought spiritual guidance. A month after Doug left her, she ran to the church in which she'd been baptized and confirmed and asked for help. A newly ordained minister spent hours talking to her. By the time Matt left her, that church had been sold, so she went knocking on the door of the church in which she and Matt had been married. Again she'd been fortunate, because this time she talked to a female minister who eventually would counsel her. She joined the church and approached Matt to tell him about the minister who did counseling and how good she was. She gave him her number just in case he wanted to see her too. A few months later, she was surprised to see him sitting in a pew for a Sunday service. That filled her heart with hope, but it was short lived.

Before she left the parking lot that day in Murdock, she offered up a prayer of thanks. She placed her hand on a metal clip on her sun visor that was inscribed with the words from Proverbs 3:5 and said, "Thank you, Lord, for getting us here safely. I hadn't even thought about driving to Murdock until I had felt a very strong urge to drive in this direction. I know that was your Holy Spirit working in me, and I thank you. It's exactly where I need to be right now to calm myself and to feel your presence. I need your help. If Matt doesn't give me some answers soon, I'll surely die. Please be with both of us during this very troubling time. Amen."

From there she drove to the downtown core and called her sister-in law, Kate, to let her know where she was, just in case there was a family emergency. Lauren considered Kate more of a sister than a sister-in-law. They had a lot in common. They both worked in the same lab and always had a lot of laughs when they were together. She told Kate that she didn't know how long she'd be staying in Murdock, but that she'd call her daily to let her know what was happening.

She headed east in search of a motel or lodge where she could stay for the night with her dog. Fortunately, she happened upon a rustic looking lodge surrounded by giant pine trees. She pulled into the parking lot to have a closer look at it. The lot had more snow machines than cars in it, and she presumed that it must be a local stop on a trail map.

She and the dog got out of the truck and headed in the direction of the flashing neon sign that read "Vacancies." It had started to snow, and in the distance she heard the roar of sleds flying down the lake and smelled the faint odor of burnt oil. Inside the lodge she could hear music playing and people laughing. She pictured a bunch of snowmobilers sitting around with glowing red faces and their suits covered in decals and zipped down to their waists. All of them would be drinking their favorite ale.

As luck would have it, they did have a room available and they had no problem with her dog staying in the room with her. She signed the register, took the key to her room, and went for a moonlit walk with her dog. She had plummeted into the depths of despair. Matt was dead to her, and she had no soft place to fall. Here she was in the middle of nowhere, completely alone with her thoughts and feelings that had gone from fear to dread. She believed that her worst fear would materialize soon. Matt, just like Doug, was going to leave her. She didn't know why, but she'd convinced herself to prepare for the worst.

She and the dog spent the next two days walking on the lake and on snowmobile trails. As she walked, she prayed for the strength to survive whatever awaited her at home. By the third day, The Weather Network was predicting a severe snow storm and high winds. They were warning motorists to stay off the roads. Concerned that she'd be snowed in, Lauren decided that she better leave and head in the direction of home.

By 6:00 a.m. she and the dog were on the road, with Lauren praying that she'd make it home safely. The roads were treacherous, and the visibility was poor. She kept on going, hoping she didn't end up in the ditch. God answered her prayers, and by 9:00 a.m. she pulled into her driveway.

The front door was unlocked. She opened it and nearly hit Matt in the face. He was standing behind the door with his coat and boots on, looking like he was rushing to get out. He said hi to her and then got down on his knees and hugged the dog.

"We need to talk right now," Lauren said. "Whatever you've been hiding, you need to tell me right now. Your silence is deadly and will kill both of us. I refuse to go down with you."

"Not now," Matt said as he picked up his gym bag. "I'm late for my spin class. I need to go."

When his hand reached the door knob Lauren screamed.

"Now! Right Now! You're not going anywhere until this is settled."

He dropped his gym bag, took off his coat and boots, and walked downstairs with Lauren behind him.

"I'm only asking you this one more time," she screamed in frustration. "Did you murder someone? Did you rob a bank? Did you have an affair?"

Instead of the three "no's" that had become his trademark response, he answered with only two "no's" this time. It seemed like hours had passed before he whispered "yes" in reference to her third question. Lauren made him repeat it, because she couldn't accept what she thought she heard. He cleared his throat and spoke again: "Yes."

Lauren sat down at the computer and remained silent for a minute or two.

"Have you ever heard the expression," she finally said, "'Hell has no fury like a woman scorned?'"

"No," he answered.

"Well, you're living it now," she screamed.

Lauren's worst fear had just materialized. Had she set herself up by anticipating that, in time, Matt would "pull a Doug" and cheat on her too, because she just wasn't enough?

18

YOU CAN'T UNRING THE BELL

Lauren tore through their home like it was on fire. In less than twenty minutes, she threw everything Matt owned into a big pile in their driveway. The snow continued to fall as he desperately tried to retrieve his very expensive skis, ski boots, golf clubs, and all the other gear he had accumulated over the years. He had to be careful where he walked, because the egg crates in which he stored his golf balls flew open as Lauren tossed them into the pile. He frantically tried to stuff everything he picked up into his car.

To make matters worse, Lauren had cut her hand badly as she was trying to rip open a storage container. Now, everything she touched had a drop or two of her blood on it. By the time she stripped every room of anything that belonged to Matt, she was exhausted and crying hysterically. She ran downstairs and collapsed into the computer chair. She put her head down on the table and sobbed so hard she could barely breathe.

She didn't know how long it was before Matt came up behind her and asked if she was okay. She screamed "no" at him and told him to stop moving her chair from left to right. He insisted that he wasn't even touching her chair, but she kept feeling it move. Years later, she could still remember the feeling of her chair moving back and forth. She felt like she was being rocked and someone was trying to comfort her.

She had no idea how long she stayed that way. Eventually she felt Kate, her sister-in-law, shaking her.

"Lauren…Lauren," Kate said worriedly. "What did you take? Sleeping pills? What drugs did you take? We have to go to the ER right now."

Lauren raised her head and screamed.

"Are you out of your mind? The only way I'm going there is if I'm in a body bag."

Kate stayed with her, hugged her, and reminded her that everything was going to be okay. At some point Lauren gathered up enough energy to ask Kate to tell Matt to get out the house and go and move in with his girlfriend. At that time, unknown to her, the girlfriend was already living with her new boyfriend. She didn't want him either.

Time moved in slow motion after that. Matt moved in with a friend of his, and Lauren stayed in their home. When the shock of the betrayal started to ease, she called every friend she had. She knew she was going to need them to help carry her through this ordeal. She asked those who prayed to pray for her. She found it difficult to pray, because she was so angry. The only purpose all that anger served was to keep enough fuel in the fire to keep her moving.

She started going to more A.A. meetings and talked and talked and talked to anyone who would listen to her. She often went to a little chapel in the city that was open twenty-four hours a day, and she resumed her counseling sessions with her favorite counselor.

Matt came by their home occasionally, and Lauren had to keep reminding him that he had to pay for half the bills. Sometimes he did and sometimes he didn't. She felt like she was the one who had wronged him and now was being held hostage in their home. It was difficult to get Matt to commit to anything because he was a busy boy. In the winter he went skiing and to the gym, and in the summer he went golfing and dragon boating. If she wanted to talk to him, he had to check his schedule before he'd make a commitment. Matt insisted that he still wanted to see the dog, but was only available between 2:00 and 5:00 because he had to nap after golfing and he had dragon boat practices in the evening. He also belonged to a gym and didn't want to miss any of the classes in which he was enrolled.

He eventually moved back into the house, but any hope that they might get back together ended on the day he told Lauren he needed to talk to her. She was sure that he was going to recommend that they go for counseling together, but that wasn't the case.

"I need your opinion," he began. "I found a nice apartment on the water that I want to move to, and I just wanted to know what you think about that?"

She couldn't believe what she had just heard.

"I think it's financial suicide," she fired back. "And if you do that, there will be no hope for us to reconcile and have a life together."

Matt seemed surprised. "I'll still come by the house occasionally," he said. "I just need some time alone."

His response enraged Lauren.

"Are you out of your mind?" Lauren screamed as loud as she could. "What are you going to do with the time that you're telling me you need? Sit in your lazy boy with a pair of binoculars watching our house? We don't need time alone right now; we need to pray like crazy, "duke it out," and work our buns off in order to either reconcile or get closure and then divorce."

His next comment almost sent Lauren looking for her father's gun. He sounded like a teenage boy who wanted the keys to his mommy's car.

"You don't understand," he whined. "I need to make a decision by tomorrow because the landlord is holding it for me. It's a really nice apartment and it has laundry facilities right in the apartment. I'd never have to go to a laundry mat. The best part is that it's on the water. The rent is $1,200.00 a month."

Lauren walked out of the room to cool off. She was sure she had steam coming out of her nostrils. Matt didn't need her blessing to get his own apartment; it was a done deal. He moved out of the house permanently the following month.

19

TESTING, TESTING

By the time Matt moved out of their home, Lauren was consumed with fear, dread, and anger. Although a lot of her anger was justified, she worried that if it got out of control, she could do something really stupid. Her counselor told her that anger invariably is based on the perception of a threat due to a conflict, injustice, humiliation, negligence, betrayal, and abandonment. Matt's betrayal fit into all those categories. It became important to Lauren to be able to identify what she was feeling and to remember that feelings can be transient and sometimes lie. She'd tried to learn how to be patient and not act as quickly as she usually did; she now gave herself time before making any major decisions.

Lauren knew that Matt had withdrawn his affection deliberately, and when he didn't pay attention to her needs or pain, she suffered intensely. She'd never met Matt's girlfriend, but she knew a lot about her, because Matt talked about her all the time. One day he called her from work to talk about a problem Jessica was having with a relative staying at her home. After an hour on the phone, Lauren reminded him that he was at work and the company was paying him to work. That day she'd felt like she was back in high school and had been listening to one of her friends who was having problems at home and needed her advice.

Lauren experienced many powerful gut feelings during that time, yet she ignored them all. One day Matt picked her up at the garage where she'd left her truck to be serviced. He was driving a new compact car, and Lauren couldn't get comfortable in the passenger seat. She tried adjusting the seat, but to no avail. As they pulled into their driveway,

Lauren asked why the seat was uncomfortable, and why it felt like she was sitting on someone. This was the car Matt drove to work in … and picked up a passenger on the way. Lauren had only been in his car once before, but Jessica had ridden in it many times. Had it just been coincidental that Lauren felt like she'd been sitting on someone that day in Matt's car?

She wasn't only angry at Matt and Jessica; she was angry at herself. How could she have been so stupid and miss the obvious? In time she forgave herself, realizing that she was only guilty of trusting her husband. It hadn't been easy for her to do, especially because her first husband had an affair and ended up married to the other woman.

Matt came by the house one day to pick up some of his belongings.

"She's really mad," he said.

"Who's mad?" Lauren asked.

Matt explained that Jessica became angry when he told her that his wife knew about the two of them. He appeared to be very upset that Jessica was upset. Lauren had a fit and told him to get off the property, because he was acting like he cared more about Jessica's feelings than he did about his wife's.

After he left, Lauren sat down in a lawn chair and pondered what had just taken place. The more she thought about it, the angrier she became. How could anyone be so cruel and self- centered? What had she done to deserve that kind of treatment? She'd been more than willing to own half the marriage; however, she was not willing to own what Matt and Jessica had done.

Lauren saw that as a sign of growth. At least she hadn't tried to take the blame for Matt's lying and cheating. He was the one who'd made the choice to cheat, and he knew before he did it that Lauren would be devastated. He put what he thought were his needs above his duties and responsibilities as a husband. It was a huge price to pay, and Lauren believed he'd sacrificed it all to have a woman he barely knew bring out the worst in him and play a role in destroying his marriage. Love had no part in their affair. Selfishness and "me first" lie at the core of infidelity. They had both been emotionally and spiritually immature, and Satan sat back and laughed as he watched them destroy their lives.

Matt's constant references to his girlfriend drove Lauren insane. Did he think he was bragging to a golf buddy or some guy he used to drink with? Lauren had way too much information on Jessica ... some of it very personal. What was Matt's reason for doing this? Lauren could easily paint a picture in her head of what the other woman looked like, because Matt often talked about how pretty she was. That isn't information a betrayed women needs to know, especially when she can barely function and looks like she hasn't slept in a month.

That day while sitting there pondering her life, she caught herself getting angrier by the moment. By the time she told herself to cool it with the "stinking thinking," she was already on her feet and in motion. She headed to the garage, which was a few hundred feet away from the house. She went in and started pacing around in a circle. The more she paced, the angrier she got. By the time she noticed Matt's shiny, expensive rims and tires leaning against the garage wall, she had become enraged. She grabbed an old filet knife from the work bench and started slashing the tires.

She stabbed the tires while yelling and screaming. Her dog was in the garage with her and started barking as if to say "Stop it! Stop it now." By the time she stopped, she was sweating and her hand was extremely sore. She lay down on the floor weeping and wailing and trying to catch her breath. As she looked up at the rafters, all she could say was, "Help Me." She didn't know if she was calling out to God for help, or if she was hallucinating and seeing a vision.

She stayed on the floor for a long time with her dog curled up beside her. All of the sudden, she jumped up and ran into the house to get her truck keys and purse. She drove up to the garage and threw the tires into the back of the truck. She and her dog headed down the driveway and stopped at the mailbox.

"Do you think I can do this?" Lauren said, looking at the dog. "Do you think we should repair those tires that I stabbed? Do you think someone is testing me to see what I'll do next?"

During her drive to the dealership, Lauren tried to convince herself that Matt deserved to have his tires wrecked, because he'd wrecked her. She started to think about what she'd learned in treatment. She was responsible to fix the wrongs she did, and if she wanted to stay sober and not live her life looking over her shoulder in fear that someone she'd hurt was behind her, she needed to apologize and make amends. She knew it would be hard to do, but the rewards were well worth it, because she'd sleep better and not drink.

She arrived at the dealership, and before she could change her mind she got out of the truck and went in to ask if they repaired tires. The man at the service counter said that they did do repairs and that he would go with her to have a look at them. He followed her to the parking lot and opened the tailgate to get into the back of the truck for a closer look at the tires.

"What happened?" he asked. "It looks like somebody had a big hate on for the tires."

"I'd rather not say," Lauren replied sheepishly. "Can you repair them?"

He assured her that he could, but it was going to cost her. Her fit of rage cost her $250.00, but it was the best money she ever spent. She was proud of herself for repairing the damage she'd done, and she planned to apologize to Matt and take full ownership for her actions. If there was a big video camera rolling in the heavens, she didn't have to worry, because she knew she'd done the right thing. She'd been tested and she passed the test, which meant she didn't have to carry the burden of guilt.

A week later, Matt came by to pick up his summer tires. Lauren explained that his tires had gone for a ride in the back of her truck. She apologized to him, but he still became angry.

"Look at it this way," she said, "I kept you out of the morgue and myself out of jail. A pretty good deal for $250.00, don't you think?"

She then turned her back on him, looked towards the heavens, and said, "Thanks, God." She left Matt checking out his tires with a magnifying glass.

20

PLEASE, DEAR LORD…
I NEED BONNIE TO BE ALIVE

It was the middle of April and the ground was still covered with snow. It had been a severe winter with a record breaking amount of snow. Lauren could see the daffodils and crocuses in her garden trying to peek through, and small areas of grass were starting to show. Spring was her favorite time of year, because its arrival carried with it the promise of hope and renewal.

Their home sat on a large piece of property with the lake on one side and a hundred acres of undeveloped land across the road from them. It was common to see deer, bear, fox, raccoon, and many different species of birds on the property. Lauren's favorite was a trumpeter swan that had taken a liking to her. She named it Grace.

Her father was the one who instilled in her a love for Jesus, and he also taught her all about God's creatures. Because of him, she grew to love all wildlife. Nothing made her happier than being outdoors. Forced into retirement because of FMS, she tried to spend as much time as possible outside. She took her camera with her and waited for the magic to happen. Without fail, she'd spot a raccoon with her babies in tow, or a white tailed deer, or a pileated woodpecker, or beautiful song birds.

One spring day, a pair of mallard ducks landed on the property while there was still snow on the ground. They left at dusk and returned early the next morning. That became their daily routine throughout the spring and summer. Sometimes they waddled up from the lake, and other times they landed at the front of the house. Their favorite spot to spend the day was under a crabapple tree on the front lawn. Lauren started throwing a handful of crushed corn onto the grass around the tree. To her surprise, the ducks loved it.

She dubbed the ducks Bonnie and Clyde. They were very vocal with each other. Clyde made the most noise. He would quack loudly whenever Bonnie waddled away from him. Obviously his job was to protect her, so if he couldn't see her, his quack became louder by the moment until she returned to him.

They were hilarious to watch, because they acted like a little old couple who'd been together forever. Bonnie was very adventuresome, but Clyde was not. He constantly fluffed up his feathers and stretched his neck out as far as it would go, quaking away and trying to ward off anything or anyone he thought was a threat to him and his "wife." Bonnie, the more laidback of the pair, often tucked her head under a wing to have a snooze. After it rained, she'd have a bath in a puddle on the lock stone at the front of the house.

One sunny summer day, Lauren saw Clyde land, but Bonnie wasn't with him. Lauren was concerned that something had happened to her. She could hear quaking in the distance, but couldn't figure out where it was coming from. Clyde didn't look too concerned as he gobbled up the crushed corn. Lauren just happened to look up and there was Bonnie, waddling around on the roof and seeming to enjoy herself. Lauren grabbed her camera and took pictures while chuckling and thinking that the couple must have had an argument, and Bonnie wasn't going to give in—even it meant that Clyde got to eat all the corn.

For the next four years, Bonnie and Clyde returned to their home in the spring. By the third week in April, Lauren would start watching for them. Without fail, they'd arrive before the end of the month. They landed in the same spot every year in a fanfare of glory, quacking loudly to announce their arrival. Lauren greeted them with, "Welcome home; you must be hungry after your long flight," and then headed in the direction of the garage to get their favorite corn as they waddled along behind her.

By the fourth year they didn't spend as much time together at their home. Some days Bonnie would be alone, and other days they'd land and have a couple of other female mallards with them. Clyde didn't seem to be paying as much attention to Bonnie as he usually did, and Lauren jokingly asked Bonnie if Clyde was seeing other women. By the end of that summer, all the visits stopped. Lauren worried that a predator had gotten them and she would never see them again.

By the following spring, everything had changed. Matt was gone and Lauren was alone. She wished that Bonnie and Clyde would return so that she could distract herself from her pain by watching the antics of the duck couple.

By the end of April, Lauren was in the depths of despair. Matt clearly wasn't interested in even talking about reconciliation. He didn't do any work at their home to try to maintain it, so she was trying to figure out a way to keep the house and not have to sell it. Fear had a grip on her, and she was struggling just to get through each day. She was afraid for her future. How could she manage by herself? Where would she move to if she needed to move? She'd never lived in the city or in an apartment, and she knew she would hate it if she was forced into it.

On one of the darkest days of her life, while walking towards the garage, she happened to look in the direction of the crabapple tree and saw something under the tree that looked like a pile of feathers. She stopped dead in her tracks, because the feathers looked eerily familiar. Her mind was racing as she stood there trying to work up enough courage to move closer. Was it Bonnie? Had she come to her summer home to die? Lauren took baby steps towards the tree and could see that whatever it was, it didn't look like it was alive. She tried to convince herself that a fox or a coyote dragged something into her yard, leaving the feathers and carcass behind.

Inch by inch she crept forward. When she realized that it was a duck, her eyes filled with tears. She couldn't see a head on the duck … just a ball of feathers. Fearing the worst, she raised her hands towards the heavens.

"Please, dear Lord," she prayed. "I need Bonnie to be alive."

As she reached the tree she was crying softly and talking to the feathers as though they were Bonnie. She reached down to make the sign of the cross on what was left of the bird, and as she did, a little head popped out from under a wing and quacked the loudest quack Lauren had ever heard.

Lauren started jumping up and down saying, "Thank you! Thank you, Lord! Bonnie is alive." She looked down at Bonnie, who was busy plumping her feathers.

"I am so proud of you," Lauren said to the duck. "You obviously weathered all storms to make it home to me. Clyde doesn't seem to be anywhere in sight, so I assume you were traveling alone. If one old mallard duck can do what you did, this old duck can do it, too. I'm going to be okay. Let's go get you some of your favorite corn from the garage. I kept some from last year, hoping that I'd see you again." Bonnie followed Lauren to the garage, quacking all the way.

Bonnie stayed close by for the summer, but Clyde never did show. By late August, the house was sold. One of the hardest things Lauren had to do was say goodbye to Bonnie. She didn't dare tell anyone what she said to her the day she left her home for good, because people would think that she was mentally unstable. She'd told Bonnie that she loved her, and she knew that God had sent her to let her know that she was going to be okay. Just like her dad had told her, if God looks after the little sparrows, she doesn't need to worry, because God will look after her, too.

When moving day arrived, Lauren put the last of the corn out on the lawn and whispered to Bonnie: "I'm moving to 142 Warren Street in the city, and there's a lake close by. Please come by for a visit. Godspeed."

Oddly enough, one day the following spring when Lauren wasn't home, Karl came by for a visit and heard ducks quaking. When Lauren returned home, Karl told her that two mallard ducks had waddled up from Warren Street onto her property and then waddled right past him back onto the adjoining street. Lauren told him that she'd given Bonnie her new address before she left the lake, so obviously she'd found her. Then she asked her brother if he'd invited them to stay and coaxed then by offering them corn? Her brother loved wildlife as much as she did, so they shared a good laugh about the country ducks that moved to the city.

21

A HANDSHAKE
AND A TOONIE

Lauren was getting desperate; something had to change. She prayed constantly that Matt would come back home so they could work on saving their marriage. She was still angry over his betrayal and had told him that she didn't condone what he'd done, but at least nobody had died. She believed that they needed to face their pain and not run away from it. She started talking about forgiveness and told Matt that it was a tough process, but it was doable. She also told him that her faith demanded that she forgive, because God had forgiven her. It was a tall order, but it was better than living with hatred in her heart.

Matt didn't say anything out loud, but his actions spoke for him. He didn't appear interested in doing anything with Lauren, but finally agreed to try counseling. He insisted that they go to the same counselor he'd gone to, and Lauren felt hopeful because he'd booked the appointment himself. Throughout the hour-long session, Matt looked bored out of his mind and said very little. All Lauren could think about was that this was the counselor Jessica had gone to who had told her to leave her husband. That may not have been true, but she couldn't get it out of her mind. As a result, she didn't trust anything he said. The whole hour was a waste of time.

Lauren went to her counselor and asked if she would counsel them as a couple. The counselor said she would, but she needed to talk to Matt first to avoid any conflict of interest. They eventually made an appointment with her, but Lauren felt like it, too, had been a waste of time because of Matt's attitude. He didn't talk about the affair or show any remorse. It was like they'd gone there to have a cup of coffee and chat about the weather. Lauren gave him the benefit of the doubt, thinking that maybe he was nervous. When she asked him if he'd join her again, he refused.

Matt's actions spoke volumes to her. The gym, dragon boating, and golfing were his priorities, and he always had time for them. He never offered to help her with any of the work required to maintain a home, and she had to remind him that bills needed to be paid.

Lauren couldn't go on the way things were. She continued to feel like a hostage in her own home. She thought it would be foolish to abandon the house, but she didn't want to stay, either. She was between a rock and a hard place. One of her biggest concerns was her health. If she didn't find a way to ease the stress of the mess she was in, she'd end up in bed all the time with every muscle in her body aching. Matt's indifference also concerned her. He didn't seem to care about what happened to his home, wife, family, or friends. The only time she saw him smile was when he was around their dog.

Lauren believed that Matt's silence and indifference were his way of controlling situations in which he didn't want to give an opinion or be involved with making a decision. She also believed that fence sitters were afraid that if they did get involved and were part of a decision making process, that they'd be blamed and punished if things didn't work out. Answering all questions with "I don't know," or "I'm not sure," or "You decide," makes the people who live with fence sitters feel like they are living in limbo. Because everything is a big secret, they never know where they stand with that person. The silence is often misinterpreted as "You're not worth talking to."

When Matt acted indifferently around Lauren after his affair, she felt like she wasn't worth talking to because he'd found someone else who was worth talking to. She didn't know if he was still seeing Jessica, or what exactly he was doing in his apartment on the water. He could have had ten women in there with him, because she'd never been inside his apartment. She was never invited to see it. It was off limits to her, and she had to wait in the parking lot for him to come down to get the dog for their visit together. She also had to wait in the parking lot of his gym for his class to be over so that he could have his prearranged visit with the dog. He'd made it very clear to Lauren that the dog was very important to him, but she was not. He needed time with the dog, but not her.

One day shortly after he moved out of the house for good, he called to say he wanted to see Flash. Lauren was in no mood to see him, so she tied the dog to a post at the front of the house and put his blanket and chew bone in a bag bedside him. The dog looked totally confused, because he'd never been tied in his life. Lauren watched through the blind on the window until she saw Matt's car coming down the driveway.

Lauren wondered about what must happen to kids of separated parents who are waiting for their mother or father to pick them up. If the child is waiting for their dad to pick them up, and their mother is in the house raging mad at their father, what messages are the parents sending to the child? She knew just by looking at her dog that even an animal is able to feel that something is wrong. Is my owner mad at me? Did I do something wrong?

Something was going to have to give if nothing changed. Lauren was aware of the fourth step of the Twelve Steps of A.A. She tried to ignore it, but it began to haunt her. The fourth step referred to conducting a searching and fearless moral inventory on oneself. She blamed everything on Matt, and she bought into the theory that he was the one, not her, who needed to do a moral inventory. She'd built walls around her ego and was standing behind those walls, swinging her club of anger. Although understandable, it wasn't right. Becoming aware of what she was doing as opposed to what Matt wasn't doing shone a new light on the whole picture.

The thought had never occurred to her that she didn't have to cater to Matt, because he'd never asked or demanded that of her. She catered to him every day of their marriage—not because she thought he expected her to, but because she was afraid if she didn't, he'd leave her. Fear controlled and motivated her every move. When her worst nightmare materialized, she upped the ante and went from fear to dread.

Fear is defined as a natural reaction or instinct; however, dread is defined as terror or apprehension. Lauren could honestly say that during that time in her life, not knowing what Matt was doing or thinking, she felt like she was the puppet and he was the puppeteer. She was being held hostage in the prison of her own mind. He wasn't holding a gun to her head, but he might as well have been, because Lauren had felt like she was a victim in a hostage taking event.

Once she learned the truth that we teach people how to treat us, she wondered what she'd taught Matt during their marriage. She concluded that she'd taught him that not much was expected of him, because she did it all. If she had to she would cut his meat in little pieces before he ate it, or peel his orange so his fingers didn't get sticky. That would have been acceptable behavior if he were a one year old. When he wouldn't do what she wanted, she'd try to control him with her silence or by yelling, which is typical behavior for a twelve year old. When she wanted to talk about emotionally charged situations, he ran away because he couldn't go there. That also had made her feel like she wasn't worth talking to.

It became obvious to Lauren that they'd been in a power struggle. They used different tactics, but both wanted and needed the same end result. When Matt cheated on her and left her, she lost all power to control him. Some of that power may have been transferred over to him, which he in turn may have given away to the other woman.

Feeling like you've lost your power in a relationship can be devastating, but even worse is giving your power away because you don't think you deserve to have any. We give our power away often, and in doing so allow other people to treat us any way they want. If Matt hadn't been able to meet his girlfriend's demands, she may have left him because of it, and that would have left him feeling powerless. The two of them may have been standing side by side in a town called Powerless and not recognized each other. If that were the case for the "other woman," she must have felt very powerful. In time, however, she'd be stripped of all the power she'd gained by giving away her integrity. What would she do then?

After conducting a moral inventory on herself instead of on Matt, she tried a different approach when talking to him. She asked God to help her find some kind of resolution to end the uncertainty in her life. The next time she saw Matt, she told him about her idea to make his life easier. That got his attention and he wanted to hear what she had to say. Before speaking, Lauren prayed silently for courage.

"Why don't you sign your half of the house over to me," she said calmly, "and then take everything else. I'll do all the legal work. You won't have to do anything except sign your name, then you'll be free to do whatever you want. You won't have to worry about paying half the bills, I'll assume any debt left on the house. I won't take you to court or sue you for any of your pension or investments. We'll close our joint bank account, and I'll take my name off all your credit cards and polices. You'll still get my hospital pension if I die before you, because even if I wanted to, I can't legally change my beneficiary. You can take anything you want from the house, and I'll clean everything up by myself if and when I sell it."

Matt remained silent, so Lauren continued.

"If we have to go to a lawyer to figure out who's going to get what, we could be ten years older and a whole lot poorer by the time things are settled."

At that point Matt turned to Lauren and put his hand out.

"Okay," he said, "you've got yourself a deal."

She shook his hand and thanked him.

Within a week, they were sitting in their lawyer's office. The lawyer asked Matt what he wanted for signing the house over to Lauren. Matt stated that he wanted a handshake and a toonie. Lauren reached into her purse to take out a coin, and then she shook Matt's hand and gave him the toonie. Matt got up and silently left the room.

"That was strange," the lawyer commented. "He doesn't want me to draw up any papers saying what he gets when he signs the house over to you."

"It doesn't look like it," Lauren replied. "I think God played a huge role in what just happened."

22

YOU HAVE TO BE KIDDING ME!

During the year prior to Matt leaving her, Lauren continued going to her counselor, Melanie. Talking openly and honestly with her helped to ease the emotional pain that she was carrying. Not only was she an excellent counselor, but she was a woman of God, and Lauren trusted her.

One day during a session, Melanie went to the blackboard and asked Lauren to tell her about her birth family and the order in which her siblings had been born. Lauren was the first born, followed two years later by her sister, Lynne, who died at three months. Warren was eight years her junior, Karl, fifteen years her junior, and Beth, seventeen years her junior. Family pictures depicted one unhappy teenager surrounded by three of her siblings. Because of the age difference, Lauren looked almost old enough to be their mother.

Melanie drew a stick person on the blackboard depicting each child. She drew a cross between Lauren and her brother, Warren, to represent the death of a child. Pointing at the cross, she asked Lauren what it had felt like for her when her brother Warren was born, because she'd been an only child for eight years.

Lauren stared at the blackboard, and after a few moments she admitted that she hadn't really liked it when her brother came home from the hospital. Melanie gently coaxed her to talk about that time in her life. She remained silent for a few moments and then the flood gates opened.

Tears ran down her face as she shared the story of the night her dad came into her bedroom and woke her up to tell her she had a brother. He'd picked her up and started dancing around the room as she sang

"Beautiful Savior." In between verses, he kept saying, "You have a brother. He's so beautiful. You'll meet him tomorrow."

Lauren continued with her story as if she had been thrown back in time and was eight years old again. She remembered feeling very confused, because nobody had said anything to her about a new baby. That night when her dad put her back in bed, he tucked her in and together they said the "Now I lay be down to sleep" prayer before he left the room. The next thing she heard was the snap of a cap coming off a bottle and her dad talking to her uncle. He was talking very loudly and saying, "I finally have a son. I'm so happy."

Lauren lay in her bed, staring at a picture on the wall of Jesus surrounded by sheep. It was a puzzle she'd received for her birthday. She and her dad had put the puzzle together and then he glued it to a board and hung it in her room. Before she closed her eyes every night, she'd look at the picture and dream of meeting Jesus and having her own flock of sheep when she grew up.

In the days that followed, Lauren had not been very happy, because Warren cried all the time. Her mom had explained to her that he had something called colic, and that he would grow out of it. Every night her dad would get Warren out of his crib and start walking back and forth in the kitchen with him. He'd be singing or talking to Warren, telling him that he would be okay. Lauren couldn't stand the noise and often didn't fall asleep unless she put her pillow over her head to drown out the sound of a crying baby.

Everything changed after Warren was born. Her dad wasn't the same any more. He used to spend every day after work with Lauren, regardless of what he was doing or where he had to go. On his payday he'd take her with him to the bank, and whatever amount of change was written on his check would go to her. On his days off, they would hunt or fish, and in the summer they spent hours together picking blueberries and exploring the bush. Her dad was also her Sunday school teacher, and she felt extra special in his class, because he'd give out candy and Lauren always got more than the other kids.

She vividly recalled being in her bedroom when she was almost three years old, screaming at the top of her lungs because her dad had just told her he had to go out of town to make some money so he could buy her nice things. She also remembered her mother peeking out from behind a curtain that hung in the doorway. After her dad had said goodbye, her mother slowly walked towards her. Lauren screamed even louder, and her dad had to come back into the room to calm her down. That would have taken place a few months after her sister, Lynne, had died. As an adult she couldn't imagine the pain that her parents must have endured during that time. Her mother may not have been emotionally ready to look after a screaming three year old when her husband had to leave to find work.

She also remembered her dad putting her in a wagon and practically running down the street with her. She could hear her mother yelling at her dad that she didn't want him to take me to the Mine Workers Club. Her dad never even looked back, and when they got to the club, he put Lauren on his shoulders and walked around to talk to all of his buddies. His friends always had a treat for her. When it was time to shoot pool, he'd put her on the edge of the table to keep an eye on her. Some days he'd bowl instead of shooting pool, so Lauren would spend her time drawing on the score cards with him beside her.

Once a month there would be boxing or wrestling events at the club, and Lauren would sit on her dad's shoulders so she could see what was going on. In the summers there were horse shoe competitions and baseball. Lauren never remembered her mother being there, but she did remember how upset her mom would be when they got home. Her dad probably hadn't eaten before they went to the club, so it wasn't uncommon for him to make french fries for the two of them at 10:00 p.m.

When she had started kindergarten, her dad would walk her to school. If he couldn't be there to take her to school and pick her up, he arranged for one of the neighbor's children, a teenage girl, to walk with her. He paid her twenty-five cents (a lot of money in 1950), and Lauren felt very important walking with the big kids. Every Saturday, her dad would take her across the street from their home to visit an elderly gentleman. In the summer, his whole backyard was filled with poppies, and each time before they'd leave she got to pick any poppy she wanted.

Lauren was so caught up in reminiscing that she forgot where she was until Melanie brought her back to reality by asking her if her parents had been emotionally available to her. Without hesitation she said that her mother hadn't been, but she was sure her father was. Then Melanie asked what it had felt like for her when her dad was giving her brother all the attention that she used to get. Lauren quickly admitted that it felt as though he didn't love her anymore. He had kicked her off the pedestal and replaced her with Warren.

Melanie then asked if Lauren thought her father had enough love in his heart for both of his children. Lauren hesitated and then answered in the affirmative. Melanie went on to explain that children don't have the cognitive power to understand what's really happening. They go by feelings. She explained that it would have been very real for her to feel like she'd been replaced by her brother. Perhaps her mother hadn't been able to cope with a crying baby, because she was still grieving Lynne's death, so Lauren's dad had tried to help out as much as he could. That wouldn't have left much time for him to do all the things that he used to do with her.

Lauren said nothing for the next five minutes.

"You mean to tell me," she finally said, "that if my dad would have woken me up the night that my brother was born and told me that he loved me very much, and that he had lots of room in his heart to love both his children, that who I became as a result of feeling like I wasn't good enough for him would never have happened?"

Melanie agreed that it could have altered the course of her life. Lauren carried that "I'm not good enough" baggage into her marriage, so it's likely that nothing her husband did for her would have made a great deal of difference. Her feelings had been programmed as a child, telling her she wasn't enough for her dad. She was emotionally stuck in her past. In her marriage she would have taught her husband how to treat her, and if she wasn't good enough for her dad, how could she be good enough for her husband?

Melanie went on to explain to her that Lauren's relationship with her brother may not have been as good as it could have been. As an eight year old, she may have unconsciously considered him to be the enemy or a threat to her. In her mind, he was the reason her father kicked her off the pedestal. Melanie said that women who've been damaged emotionally as children often grow up to be people pleasers. They are driven by fear and spend a lot of time and energy looking for someone … anyone … to love and accept them.

Lauren sat there with a stunned look on her face.

"You have to be kidding me," she blurted out. "If my dad had said to me that night that I was his number one daughter and Warren was his number one son, and that he had enough love for both of us, my reaction would have been completely different? I wouldn't have been so fearful and worked my buns off trying to please everyone and prove that I was loveable? If that's the case, my life took a different course all because of a few words!"

"That's a possibility," Melanie responded. "However, if one parent is emotionally available for the child, the effects may not be as serious. If both parents are emotionally unavailable for the child, the consequences can be very damaging to the child."

Lauren asked about children who have been beaten and/or sexually abused. Her childhood was a walk in the park compared to that. She knew that nothing her father or mother had done or said was intended to harm her, yet she'd gone into the world feeling like she wasn't good enough for anyone.

"Those kids have to pray and work very hard to overcome and forgive those who have inflicted pain on them."

23

BLESS THEM AND GIVE THEM PEACE

Once Matt signed the house over to Lauren, everything changed. She knew that she was going to have to sell it, because it was too much of a financial burden and she couldn't do all the maintenance by herself. When her first husband left her she was only twenty-seven years old, and she'd worked extra hard to keep that house running smoothly. Now that she was sixty-one, she didn't have the kind of stamina that was necessary to do all the work by herself.

If Matt gave her any hope that he was going to return home, she'd find a way to keep the house. He made it very clear to her by his actions, however, that he had no intention of coming back or working on reconciliation. He seemed to have created a new life for himself, which included driving a new vehicle and sporting a new look. That was a hard pill to swallow, because she looked like she needed sleep and felt like she was walking around in a thick fog. Her fibromyalgia was acting up because of the stressful situation, and every muscle in her body was screaming at her.

She tried to keep the house in some kind of running order, just in case she had to sell it. Karl was a big help and came by often to cut the grass and do whatever else she needed done. If she didn't have her faith to fall back on, she was sure she'd start drinking again and end up in a ditch somewhere. Prayer saved her. She prayed constantly that God's will for her would be done and that He would guide and direct her to a safe place to start all over again.

A month after Matt took what he wanted out of the house, Lauren called a realtor she knew and asked him to list the house. Two weeks later, a For Sale sign was placed at the road by her mailbox. It was a bittersweet moment to see that sign being pounded into the ground. Lauren was extremely sad, yet in a small way she was also excited about the possibility of a new adventure. It was the beginning of a new life for her without Matt. Selling her house was very symbolic for her. It meant that she was willing to move forward and leave the past behind her. She was willing to do whatever it took to build a new life one brick at a time.

The difficult part about leaving the past behind was not the physical move but the emotional move. If she carried all that negative emotional baggage Matt had left her with into her new life, she was sure she would live a miserable existence. If that were the case, then moving would have been a complete waste of time and money. It wouldn't matter where she lived, or who she was with, or how much money she had; her unresolved anger would trickle down to anyone she came in contact with. Unresolved anger would also interfere with her relationship with God, and it would make her sick and send her to the grave prematurely.

Her unforgiving spirit wouldn't change just because she changed her address. Even though she had twenty years of sobriety and many hours of counseling under her belt, moving to a new home or a new country wouldn't change anything. She needed to do the work necessary to learn how to let go of her past by forgiving those who'd hurt her.

Coming out of rehab, she'd been determined to be the best she could before she left this world. This meant unlearning old behaviors by giving her will and her life over to God. Things couldn't be her way anymore, and every time she tried doing life her way, she messed up. If she wanted a whole new way to live, she'd have to learn how to recognize the guidance of the Holy Spirit.

She learned that when a person believes in Christ, the Holy Spirit immediately becomes a permanent part of their life. Lauren likened it to the still, small voice inside of her that immediately warned her when something wrong. If she didn't heed the warning and went ahead and did it anyway, she immediately knew that it was wrong. Consequently, when she did something wrong she had to apologize for her behavior and never do it again, otherwise she'd live with the burden of guilt and shame until she made it right. If she never made it right and stuffed it instead, it would never go away. In her attempt to hide it, she'd constantly need to be looking over her shoulder to see if the person she injured was behind her. Burden upon burden is like carrying a whole bunch of rocks in your backpack twenty-four hours a day. Eventually your back becomes stooped and you lose all hope of ever standing tall again.

If Lauren wanted to change, she'd have to find a way to recognize what she owned and fix the wrong she'd done. She would have to hold herself accountable and ask not only the people she'd hurt to forgive her, but God as well. He had to be included in her daily life, which meant every day of the week, not just Sundays.

She soon found out that asking for forgiveness was a difficult and humbling thing to do. Admitting that she was wrong was not an easy task. It became obvious to her that she didn't know much about forgiveness, other than saying she was sorry. She read as much as she could and asked many questions so that she could prepare herself to have a better understanding about the journey of forgiveness.

When we forgive, we aren't glossing over or denying the seriousness of the offense against us, and we aren't forgetting, condoning, or excusing it either. Forgiveness empowers us to recognize the pain we suffered without letting the pain define who we are. Forgiveness is a conscious and deliberate decision to release feelings of resentment and vengeance towards the person or group that hurt us, whether they deserve it or not. The Bible is very specific when it talks about forgiveness. We are told that we must forgive, no matter the offense, because God forgives us when we ask in His name.

In Matthew 6:14, Jesus says *"For if ye forgive men their trespasses, your heavenly Father will also forgive you."* Lauren was no theology scholar, but she took that to mean that if she didn't forgive Matt, God wouldn't forgive her. If that were the case, Matt would still have power over her if she didn't forgive him. She wouldn't be able to live a joyous and peaceful life if God refused to forgive her of her sins because she hadn't forgiven Matt. She'd take her unforgiven sins with her to the grave.

It all came down to how prepared she wanted to be to meet her Maker. Getting into Heaven wasn't conditional on how many people she forgave, or on how many amends she made, but she figured it wouldn't look good on her if she'd never forgiven anyone or asked God to forgive any of her sins. That would mean that she'd lived her life saying she was a Christian, but with no proof to back that up, because she'd never acted or spoken like one. When we believe in God, we're expected to act accordingly by being doers and not just hearers of His Word. It's about proving to God how grateful we are that Jesus died for all our sins.

Jesus laid down His life down as a voluntary act for our salvation. He died the death that all humans deserve, because we have all sinned. An exchange took place the day he died. He took our sin and gave us back peace, righteousness, and eternal life in return. However, repentance and faith must occur before the exchange of sin for righteousness happens. He died for all, but unfortunately not all have been willing to receive that gift.

Lauren spent a lot of time pondering what she'd learned about forgiveness. She decided that if God was willing to forgive her, and she was willing to accept that forgiveness, that it would be very hypocritical of her not to forgive the ones that had hurt her. Jesus was spit on, tortured, and nailed to a cross for her sins. The pain that she suffered was only a minuscule droplet of blood in a bucket compared to Jesus' five liters of blood that was all over the ground, on his body, on the cross, and on clubs and spears the day he was crucified.

On the day Lauren made the conscious choice to forgive anyone that had hurt her, she took out the toolbox she'd received when she was in rehab. On the outside of the box she'd glued her "Pass it On/Proverbs 3:5" card. She had three books inside that box, along with a pin with an acorn on it. She had her Bible, her A.A. big book, and her New Beginnings book from her counselor.

All three books had similar messages in them: love your neighbor as yourself, forgive before the sun goes down, pray constantly, don't lie or cheat or steal, pray really hard and work even harder, practice gratitude daily, don't judge people because you too will be judged one day, get out of yourself, make amends to prove you're sorry, honor your father and mother, be kind to all, help those in need, pray for those that have hurt you, honor your marriage, clean up your act, earn your money honestly, and spread the word that there is hope for all no matter what horrible thing they've done. Everyone is worthy of being forgiven by God and man. All three books gave the same warning: "Don't put off until tomorrow what you know needs to be done today. Eternity could be only one breath away. Where do you want to move to after you die to this world? You only have two choices."

There was no doubt in Lauren's mind that God was responsible for her crossing paths with Harry W. at that A.A. meeting. He told her that he prayed for people that had hurt him and asked God to bless them. After that meeting, she told herself that there would never be a time when she would be able to do that. She was too proud and too stubborn to be willing to humble herself enough to ask God to bless her enemies.

Harry had been on her mind the day she drove to the church where she and Matt had been married. She'd convinced herself that the best thing she could possibly do was to "get out of herself" and volunteer to do work around the church, instead of sitting around at home waiting for her house to sell. When she became a member there, she noticed that it looked like it could use a little sprucing up. She spoke to the minister who'd counseled her, and she was more than happy to accept Lauren's offer of help. She gave Lauren a key so that she could come and go as she pleased.

Lauren did want to help clean things up at the church, but she had an ulterior motive for wanting to be there. She wanted access to the sanctuary, when no one was around, to see if she could humble herself enough to kneel at the altar and ask God to bless Matt and give him peace. If she could manage to do that, then she'd try asking God to bless Jessica and give her peace, too. She knew it wouldn't be coming from her heart if she had to force herself to do it; however, she believed that if she tried it would be a good sign that she was willing to start a journey of forgiveness. After many attempts, she finally knelt at the altar.

"Dear Lord," she said through clenched teeth, "please bless Matt and give him peace." When she opened her eyes, she felt a tingling of relief. She kept on doing it until it felt like the words were coming from her heart. It took her many more tries before she could ask God to bless the other woman.

She went to the church as often as she could. One day when she was carrying mops and pails out to her car, a man came up to her.

"So, you're a cleaning lady now," he said.

Lauren had an eerie feeling about him. "No," she responded, "I've just been helping to clean up and organize a few rooms."

After the stranger walked away, Lauren stood there momentarily thinking about what he had said. It sounded like he knew her from somewhere—otherwise he wouldn't have implied that she hadn't always been a cleaning lady.

Driving home she had a very uncomfortable feeling about that stranger. Had she met him before? Why did he seem to know her? Why did she feel like she should be afraid of him? What were her instincts trying to tell her? By the time she arrived home she'd forgotten all about him and wouldn't think about him again until she became aware that someone was stalking her.

24

TRY BEING GRATEFUL
FOR A CHANGE

Small miracles began to happen to Lauren. Her home sold and she was offered a very generous price. She managed to give away all the stuff Matt left behind, and she had all her belongings organized and ready to go. The only problem was that she hadn't been able to find a home to move to. She was fortunate that the buyers of her home offered a closing date that gave her eight weeks to find a place to live. She was confident that she could find something in that time, and if not, she and her dog could move to an apartment.

She spent as much time as she could driving around the city to look at houses. Nothing looked right for her until one day when she drove down a street a block away from where she used to work and a block from the most beautiful park in the city, which happened to be on the water. She parked her truck and sat looking at the outside of the house. She had a gut feeling that it might be the one she could call home. While looking around at the other homes close by, she happened to look up and saw, to her surprise, the cross on top of the hospital she had worked in. At night, that cross would be lit up for the entire world to see. If she bought this house, it would be an added bonus to see the cross from her front window.

She called the realtor and told him she wanted to see the house at 142 Warren Street. By 5:00 p.m., she was inside and knew there would be a lot of work to do, but it felt right. She told the realtor to make an offer on it. By 9:00 p.m., her offer was accepted and she had a place to move to. She thought that it had been an odd coincidence to find a home on Warren Street, because the birth of her brother Warren had altered the course of her life when she was eight years old. Would this house alter the course of her life, too?

Moving day came and went. On the first night in her new home, all her dog wanted to do was go outside. Each time he asked to go out, Lauren followed him. He'd get as far as her car, and then sit and whine like he wanted to get in and go home. At midnight, she picked him up and carried him into her bedroom and put him on her bed. When she got in, he snuggled as close to her as possible and put his head on her as if to say he would take a bullet for her if necessary. They stayed that way for the whole night.

In the morning, she called a business in town where unemployed men gathered when they needed work. Lauren asked if they had anyone willing to break up cement and haul it into a dumpster. They said that they did and would drop two men off at her house by 10:00 a.m., but she would be responsible to pay them at the end of the day. They arrived at 10:05 and introduced themselves as Nick and Billy.

Lauren put them to work right away and explained to them that she was going to be putting down new lock stone at the side of the house. She needed them to remove all the old cement by hand, because a machine wouldn't have room to get in there. Both of the men were hard workers, and by the end of the day she was pleased at the amount of work they had done. When she asked them if they would continue to work for her, they both agreed. For the next month, she was able to keep them employed.

During that time, she got to know them both. She seemed to relate better to Billy than to Nick. When Billy told her that he was an alcoholic, Lauren wasn't surprised; she had guessed that he probably was. Some days she could smell liquor on him, and his hands had a slight tremor, but he always did the work. She paid him well and often gave him a ride home at the end of the day.

One day when she was driving him home, she mentioned to him how much she liked older homes because they had so much character. In response, he asked her if she would like to see the inside of the old house he lived in. She said yes.

"Your tour guide awaits you," he said when they arrived. "Lets' go."

Walking around in the building, Lauren felt sick to her stomach. There was filth everywhere, and the smell of urine permeated the rooms. Billy didn't seem to be embarrassed by any of that, and he proudly opened the door to show her his room. All he had was a mattress on the floor, two shaky looking chairs, an overflowing ashtray, and empty beer cases piled high in all corners. The house had a shared kitchen and washroom.

When Lauren got back into her car, she used her hand sanitizer to try to disinfect her face, arms, and hands. When she got home, she had a shower and washed the clothes she'd been wearing. She was so appalled by what she saw, and she couldn't understand how anyone could live with so much filth around them. Soap and water didn't cost much.

After that visit, Lauren asked Billy if he or anyone else who lived in his building would like to go to church with her. He said he would, so she explained to him that she would give him a ride to church on Sundays, but if he was drunk when she got there to pick him up, he was on his own.

He seemed to like going to church, and he especially liked the snacks and food served after the service. After church she drove him home. Often there was a party going on in the driveway where he lived. Everyone appeared to be high or drunk, and they were loud and out of control. Lauren often got out of her car and asked each person if they wanted to join Billy when she picked him up for church the following Sunday.

Eventually Lauren knew all their names. She noticed that one person, Norm, seemed to be running the show. She never saw him with a bottle or glass in his hand, but every time he saw her, he offered her one of the pamphlets he had in his shirt pocket. She would take one and then he would start ranting and raving about hell and damnation, and how they were all going to die. Lauren found it strange that everyone stopped talking and almost stood at attention whenever Norm the pamphlet guy was yelling and screaming. No one challenge him or asked him any questions until he finished his propaganda speech. He appeared to have power over everyone. The next time Lauren saw Billy, she asked him about Norm and why everyone seemed to be afraid of him.

Billy said that Norm was a mental case, and everybody did what he told them because he was always doing stupid things like setting a mattress on fire and trying to burn down the building. When Lauren had asked if he was on medication, Billy explained that he was supposed to take his meds because he was crazy, but most of the time he didn't.

After Nick and Billy finished the projects at her home, she told them that when she needed them again, she would call the center downtown and ask specifically for them. She was glad to see them go, because Nick had been telling her some tall tales about his brother's connection to the Hell's Angels, and she didn't like what she had been hearing. She took Billy aside and told him she would pick him up for church if he still wanted to go, and she would pray for him. She also told him that she'd asked her husband to do some of the work to help her out, but she didn't know if he was going to do it or not. If her husband didn't show up, she would contact Billy.

Matt eventually did come by to do a few things, but Lauren always felt like he didn't want to be around her, let alone help her. He was very guarded and made her feel uncomfortable. Sometimes she saw him sitting in a pew at church, and she never knew if she should sit beside him or not. The only person who knew about their separation was the minister, and she presumed that people would wonder why they weren't sitting beside each other if they were husband and wife. To save him from embarrassment, she sat beside him, but she always felt like there was a glass wall between them. She could see him, but she couldn't touch him.

Whenever Lauren had a chance to talk to Matt, she told him that if nothing changed, she would have to think about divorcing him, because it wasn't right to keep on faking it. She also couldn't continue to take advantage of his medical coverage from work. They weren't together, so how could she in good faith make a dental claim and pretend that she was still his wife. She knew that legally she was still his wife, but she needed to be able to act like she was, and she needed him to act like he was still her husband.

Matt never said a word to her when she mentioned divorce. She hoped that he would say they should give it some time and try to work on reconciling before they even thought about divorce, but that never happened.

She felt like a mother with a son in college. He would call and ask how to make the big cookies that she used to make him, or how to wash one of his good sweaters. Sometimes he just wanted to pick the dog up to go for a walk with him. At one point during their separation he went out West on a vacation. When he returned, they agreed to meet at a local park to walk the dog together. She hadn't seen him in weeks and was excited about the prospect of talking to him, hoping that being away had helped him make a decision to come back home. He crushed her dreams within five minutes.

He exited his vehicle and made a big fuss when the dog ran towards him, but all she got from him was a casual "hi." He walked by her vehicle, kicked the front tire, and said that it was going to need air in it. Then he kept right on walking. It would have been a big help had he gotten his tire gauge and checked the tire for her, but that never happened. She spent the next thirty minutes listening to him complain about how angry he was at his insurance company because they refused to pay the $30.00 it cost him to buy some Nicorette.

At that point Lauren was paying $130.00 a month for minimum health insurance coverage, because she had told him to take her off his work plan insurance. She told Matt that he should try acting grateful for a change. He had a plan that he didn't have to pay for. He never said a word and almost jogged back to his vehicle. When she finally caught up to him, he hugged the dog and then got into his car. He looked at himself in the mirror, adjusted his hat, and sped off.

Lauren didn't leave the park right away; instead, she sat there praying that God would take her pain away. She didn't know how much longer she could endure Matt's emotional abuse. She asked herself why she kept setting herself up to be hurt over and over again. Did she like being beat up emotionally? Did she still feel like she wasn't enough for Matt? Why was she still giving him permission to disrespect her and treat her any way he wanted to? Her biggest question was why did all the pain she endured as a result of his betrayal feel like a walk in the park compared to the pain she now appeared to be willing to endure.

25

THE SCARY GIFTS

Lauren kept working away at trying to make her house into a home. She was beginning to like living in town, and she really liked being so close to the park. She and her dog went for a walk there every day. The best part was that she could see the cross atop the hospital from her front window. It was like she had a giant cross watching over her twenty-four hours a day.

One day when she went back to her car to retrieve a bag she'd forgotten in the trunk, she noticed a grocery bag tied to her driver's side mirror. Her first thought was that perhaps she had dropped a bag when she was unloading her car after shopping and a kind neighbor had picked it up and tied it to her mirror. When she opened the bag, she found what looked like a gift wrapped in tissue paper. Inside the paper was a wooden plaque with Psalm 23 inscribed on it. The plaque didn't look new, because it was scratched and stained. She stared at it, wondering if someone who knew about her recovery and her faith was having a difficult time and felt like they were walking through the shadow of death. Maybe they were too afraid to come back and talk to her and had left it as some kind of symbol of hope.

She kept the gift, but because it was so dirty, she double wrapped it in plastic bags and put it in her shed. In the days that followed, she forgot all about it until another gift showed up, this time in her mailbox. It had the same "modus operandi" as the first gift. It was a crinkled and stained piece of paper that looked like it had been ripped out of some kind of devotional booklet. It talked about how we can't outgive God. It was dated July 18—exactly one month from the day she received it.

Lauren wrapped it in two plastic bags and stored it along with the Psalm in her shed. After that incident she became more cautious when she took the dog outside before going to bed. She turned all the flood lights on and made sure she had a flashlight and a small knife in her pocket. Every time she walked by her car, she checked to see if there was a bag tied to her mirror.

Nearly a month passed. She was starting to relax a little and had stopped constantly looking in her mailbox or running outside to look at the mirrors on her car, but then another gift arrived. It was in her mailbox again, and this time it looked like it had been ripped out of the same booklet as the previous one. The page was crinkled up and stained just like the previous one, except this one talked about hell and damnation and was dated August 18.

She was so scared that she called her friends and told them the story of the mysterious gift giver. They all suggested that she call the police. That made no sense to Lauren. What would the police be able to do? They couldn't charge someone for leaving her gifts. Months later, she found out that her friend who worked shift work at the hospital drove by her place every night to see if she could spot a stranger near her house. Another friend of hers, the owner of Jimmy's Sports Bar, did the same thing around 3:00 a.m. after he had locked up his bar. Lauren was so touched by their kindness that it made her realize just how important her friends were to her. They were people who would go out of their way just to help her.

When another gift arrived on September 18, she put rubber gloves on to open it up and found yet another page from the same booklet. This one talked about the fiery furnaces of hell. Lauren became hysterical and ran around checking all the locks on the doors and windows. When she worked up enough courage, she ran outside and moved her car to a place where she could keep an eye on it from the kitchen window. Before she went to bed, she checked and rechecked the alarm system, and she locked herself and her dog in the bedroom for the night. She went to bed with her cell phone, her landline phone, her knife, emergency numbers, and one bullet for her dad's .410 that was under her bed. She was too afraid to leave a bullet in the gun, because she remembered her dad's warning to make sure that there were no bullets in a gun when she stored it.

On the night that her house alarm sounded at 4:00 a.m., she grabbed the gun and put that one bullet she slept with into it. She sat on the edge of the bed, clinging to the gun and her cell phone, feeling like she was frozen to the bed. She knew that she had to turn off the alarm before it woke up everyone in the neighborhood, but she couldn't move. All she could do was pray, so she kept praying for help until she finally dialed 911. Once she knew that the police were on their way, she worked up enough courage to turn the alarm off.

Two young police officers were at her door five minutes later. After she told them about the gift giving stranger, they conducted a thorough search inside and out and found no windows or doors unlocked. They assured her that all was well. They also suggested that she call the company that looked after her alarm system. They told her to call them back if she was still afraid.

After that night she felt like she was working for a forensic lab. When she noticed some cigarette butts close to her car, she put on rubber gloves and put the butts in a plastic bag and stored them in her shed with all the other evidence she had. In bold black letters she wrote on the storage box: "Evidence from the Anonymous Gift Giver." She theorized that if ever she were to go missing or found dead, the police would have some evidence that a crime had been committed.

Matt still came by occasionally to visit with the dog. When she had told him how afraid she was, he ignored her and talked about himself. She felt that he didn't care if she were dead or alive, as long as the dog was okay. He was always talking about how busy he was, and he seemed to be quite happy being the bachelor he professed to be. Any time she mentioned to him that if something didn't change, she was going to have to file for a divorce, he ignored her and walked away. His actions and behavior began to speak very loudly for his lack of words. It painted a clear picture for Lauren. Obviously he didn't think she was worth talking to … nor was she worth the energy it took to protect her from the idiot who was leaving her gifts.

Lauren had no doubt that if she filed for a divorce, Matt—and just about everyone else— would believe that she'd filed on the grounds of adultery, even though that wouldn't be the case. She would file because he adamantly refused to participate in any kind of reconciliation after his affair. Even if they didn't stay married, they both would have gained by working out why their marriage had fallen apart. Obviously it was okay with him to still call himself Lauren's husband if he wanted to, but it wasn't okay with her. There was nothing husband-like about his actions or behavior. The Bible says that husbands are to be leaders, providers, protectors, and companions.

Lauren admitted that she wasn't a perfect wife. Her only saving grace may have been her willingness to help Matt become the best he could be, so that as a couple they could become the best they could be. She believed that their marriage had been heading for the ditch long before his affair.

Their marriage worked as long as they both were drinking. Lauren believed that once she came out of rehab, Matt sensed the change in her and that scared him. When one person in a relationship starts acting differently, the other person usually becomes confused and scared because something has changed. They often think that they must have done something wrong to cause that change in their partner.

Lauren returned home from rehab with a plan that would allow her, if she followed it, to replace drinking with something else. She replaced drinking with working through a program. She believed that when Matt quit drinking, he didn't have a plan in place that would fill the void that was left. It was only through sheer will power that he didn't drink anymore. Lauren believed that his choice to quit drinking may have been a testimonial of his love for her.

The great divide between them led them down different roads. Even though they both wanted and needed the same thing, they didn't work together to get there. They each drove their own bus on the same highway and were racing to the same destination. The only possible way their marriage could work was if they both were on the same bus with God as the driver.

In the end, it was very sad. They both had what it took to have a loving and solid marriage, but neither of them was aware of how very important it was to travel the highway of life together.

26

THE JESUS PICTURE JOURNEY

L auren thought a lot about the mysterious person who was leaving her gifts. She wasn't sure why she hadn't noticed sooner that when he left a gift, he marked it with the date on which the next gift would arrive. Following this pattern, another gift was due to arrive on October 18.

She spent that day at home, checking her mailbox and her car every five minutes, but no gifts arrived and she didn't see anyone suspicious hanging around. She took that as a good sign; maybe the person was tired of the game and had moved on to terrorize someone else. The next day saw nothing unusual, but she was unprepared for what happened the following day.

She went out and returned home just before dark, once again forgetting something in her car. It couldn't have been more than five minutes before she walked back out to her car. There it was—another bag tied to the driver's side mirror. She immediately felt a surge of adrenalin rush through her body as her heart began to race. Her feet wouldn't move, so she started silently chanting: "Fear no evil. Fear no evil. Fear no evil." All of the sudden she felt empowered and sprang into action. She ran to her car, untied the bag on her mirror, and ran for safety.

She kept looking over her shoulder as she ran. When she reached the spotlight in front of her house, she ripped the bag open and out fell a picture of Jesus. She dropped it like it was a hot piece of coal and ran into the house. She took the .410 out from under the bed, grabbed a bullet, and put it in her pocket. She then went to the phone and dialed Matt's number. Surely he would come and help her; he only lived five minutes away. He answered on the third ring. She told him what had just happened and begged him to come to the house. He told her that he was tired and had to get up early the next morning. She kept begging, so eventually he reluctantly said that as soon as he could, he would come over.

By the time he arrived forty-five minutes later, she had worked herself into a panic state and was hyperventilating. He walked in and asked what she wanted him to do.

"Please stay with me," she begged. "I'm in danger; whoever is doing this is close by."

"There's really not much I can do," Matt said. "Why don't you call the police?"

Just as Matt finished talking, the phone rang. It was Mary, the minister from her church, calling to see how she was. Lauren had asked people at her church to pray for her safety. A week earlier, Mary had been unable to reach her by phone, so she drove over to see if she was okay. Mary also told Lauren that a stranger had been asking about her at a Friday night service. She thought it would be a good idea for Lauren to inform the police about this, because the stranger appeared disorientated and wouldn't talk or tell anyone his name.

Lauren told Mary about the Jesus picture tied to her car mirror. She then had asked Lauren if she was alone in house. When told that Matt was there, she asked to speak with him. Mary told Matt that he needed to stay with his wife because she was so afraid. After the call Matt passed this along to Lauren. He had made it sound like he was being forced into staying with her, but at that time she didn't care what he thought, because she knew that she couldn't be alone.

When she'd dropped the Jesus picture after opening the grocery bag, her heart had started racing and she could taste that metal taste in her mouth that was associated with being terrified. The picture looked exactly like the picture that had been hanging on the living room wall when she bought the house. The day she moved in, she took it down because the frame looked so old and faded. She decided to store it until she had the time to fix it. She had put it in a closet upstairs along with other frames that she wanted to sand and stain.

When Matt arrived she went outside to get the Jesus picture. Once again she put rubber gloves on before picking it up and putting it into a plastic bag. Looking at it inside, she was sure that it was the same picture and frame she had stored upstairs in the closet upstairs. The age of the frame and picture made it easily identifiable. She was afraid to go by herself to check if it was still in the closet, so she asked Matt to go upstairs with her.

She remembered exactly where she had put it, but it wasn't there. All of the other frames where there, except for the one she needed to find. She frantically searched every closet upstairs, but to no avail. She didn't know who would believe her story that her Jesus picture had been stolen from her house.

Matt didn't say anything as he watched her pacing back and forth like she had a big decision to make. Within minutes, she told him that she thought Billy, the guy who had worked for her, may have had something to do with that picture. She went on to explain that the week before, she had hired Billy to do some painting for her. She told him about the gifts that kept showing up at her house, and asked him if he had any idea of who might be responsible for doing that. She thought it may have been Nick, but Billy informed her that Nick had left town with the Hell's Angels. Billy said that he thought it was Matt, her husband, because he looked like the kind of guy who would do something like that … just to scare her.

Lauren suggested to Matt that the two of them go to Billy's place to see if he could add anything more to the story. Matt declined and said he was staying put with the dog. Lauren was hurt that Matt didn't even try to discourage her from going to the sleaziest part of town at midnight. She realized that he couldn't care less what she did. That anger fuelled the fire inside of her, so she grabbed her coat and keys and off she went into the night.

She parked in front of Billy's place and found it to be eerily quiet. She expected that a huge party would be underway in the driveway. She got out of her car, praying that God would keep her safe, and walked quickly to the front door. It was locked, so she started pounding on it as hard as she could. Within minutes, a scantily glad girl who looked no older than sixteen answered the door and asked Lauren what she wanted.

"Where's Billy?" Lauren asked.

"You mean that old drunk? He's gone with some of his women to Trippers Den. Don't bother waiting for him, because he'll be as drunk as a skunk if and when he makes it back here alive."

Lauren considered going to Trippers, but she didn't know where it was, so she decided to go back home.

As she pulled away, a taxi drove up so she stopped to see if it was Billy returning home. Two young women in bikinis hopped out of the back seat of the cab. They appeared to be dragging somebody out with them. Whoever it was landed face down on the ground. The girls tried to roll the person in the direction of the house. Lauren jumped out of her car.

"Hey," she yelled. "Is that Billy?"

"Yep," one of them answered.

Lauren ran towards them.

"Billy," she yelled. "It's me, Lauren. Wake up; I need to talk to you."

Both girls started giggling.

"You're wasting your time, lady," one of them said. "You'll be lucky if he ever wakes up."

Realizing that Billy was too drunk to know what was going on, Lauren gave the girls strict orders to make sure that once they managed to get him into the house, they rolled him onto his side and put something behind him so he wouldn't choke on his own vomit and die. As she was walking away she heard one of them say, "Sure, lady. Who do think I am … his babysitter?"

She drove away and prayed that God would keep Billy safe and restore him to sanity. When she got home, Matt was on the couch and looked like he was sleeping. She called the dog to come with her and they went into her bedroom and locked the door. She put the gun back under her bed and took her phones and knife to bed with her. She prayed that night that God would restore her to sanity, and she thanked Him for keeping her safe.

27

WALKING THROUGH
THE VALLEY

Lauren didn't get out of bed until 8:00 the morning after Matt's sleepover on the couch. He was nowhere to be found and there was no note to indicate where he might have gone. It had become routine for her to check all three doors to make sure they were still locked, and that day was no different. On this occasion, though, she found door number three unlocked. She whistled for her dog, grabbed her cell phone, and ran outside.

All she could think about was someone hiding out upstairs or in the basement of her home. Maybe Matt left the door unlocked on purpose when he left that morning. Billy's suggestion that Matt was the one terrorizing her had left her questioning if it was even possible that he might be right. The more she thought about it, the more sense it made. If she was out of the picture, he'd get her pension and everything else. He was still her husband, and she hadn't made any changes to her will since he left her.

The more she thought about it, the more afraid she became. She knew that she wasn't going back into the house without someone with her. She felt like she had no other choice but to call the police. She dialed 911, and the operator told her not to go back into her house but to wait outside for the police to arrive. Within ten minutes, two police cruisers pulled up and one uniformed police officer and two plainclothes officers walked towards her.

They introduced themselves and asked her what the problem was. She gave them the whole story about the gift giver and told them that she had collected some evidence. When they asked to see it, she retrieved the box from the shed and put it down on the table in front of them. The detective in the group chuckled and jokingly said that his boys in the crime lab didn't do as good a job with evidence as she had done. Lauren cracked a smile and told them that old habits die hard. She had worked in a hospital lab, and precision and detailing were very important when analyzing a patient's blood.

When they asked if she lived alone in the house or if she had a husband, she told them that she had a husband in name only because he'd left her and now lived in an apartment only five minutes away from there. When they asked if there had been trouble in the marriage, she told them about Matt and Jessica's affair.

The officers asked permission to look around in her house. Two officers went inside, but the detective stayed behind. When the uniformed officer came out, he said all was clear and then asked why there were pictures drawn in chalk all over the exposed rock in her basement. She explained to them that recently when her minister and her children had come by for a visit, it had been raining and the children couldn't go outside to play. She'd brought them downstairs and given them chalk to draw pictures on the rock. The kids loved it because the rock was a fun blackboard. They got very creative and drew pictures of churches and printed things like "Jesus Loves You" on the rock. Lauren explained to the officers that she hadn't washed it off because every time she went down to do laundry the pictures made her feel hopeful. It was the simplicity of what those children had drawn that helped her remember the words from Psalm 8:2

The officers asked her questions about who she thought may be trying to scare her. She told them about Nick and Billy working for her, and that Nick had often talked about his brother's connection to the Hell's Angels. They asked if she had an address or phone number for the men, and she was able to tell them where they lived. They also wanted to know more about Matt. She gave them as much information as she could, including his address and phone number.

They asked to take the evidence box with them, which was fine with Lauren. Before leaving, they instructed her to keep all her doors and windows locked and to call them when she was afraid or had any more information. They gave her a card with one of the officer's direct lines on it. She thanked them and they were gone.

In the months that followed no more gifts arrived, and Lauren began to relax a little— until another mysterious package showed up in her mailbox a week before Christmas. She recognized it immediately because it was wrapped exactly the same as all the other gifts. This time it was a tiny wooden fireplace with stockings hanging from the hearth. It looked like it may have been an ornament for a tree. The message on a crumpled piece of paper talked about salvation and was dated November 20. The stranger had changed things up and was now going backwards with the dates.

Lauren didn't call the police to tell them about the latest gift. She decided that she was going to pray constantly that God would reveal the name of the stranger to her. She eventually decided that in the spring she would sell her house and move as far away from there as she could. The stranger had succeeded in filling her heart and mind with fear. The fear controlled her every move, and the worst part was that she didn't have a clue who her enemy was. It was like fighting someone with a blindfold on.

Whenever she saw Matt she watched his every move. He told her that he often saw a police cruiser parked in front of his building, and he felt like they were watching him. She still wondered if he was the gift giving stranger, and if so, how she could prove it.

In the New Year she called her lawyer to inquire about filing for a divorce. Matt showed no interest in even talking about reconciliation, and whenever she brought up the topic, he would walk away from her. Although she occasionally saw him at church and sat beside him during the service, she still felt like nobody was home. He acted aloof and cold whenever she saw him.

28

THE SHADOW OF DEATH

In March of that year, Lauren went to her lawyer and got all the information she needed to file for a divorce. She called Matt and told him what she'd done and asked him if he wanted to talk about it. He refused, saying that she could do whatever she wanted.

When she made the decision to follow through with a divorce, she called Matt again to tell him that she'd booked an appointment with their lawyer, and that the following Monday she was going to file for an uncontested divorce. She hoped and prayed that he would stop her by saying that they should give it a little more time, but he said nothing except that he hoped it went well for her. When Monday arrived she still had a glimmer of hope that he would be standing at her lawyer's office door insisting that she not divorce him. It never happened, and by noon of that day she was well on her way to the title of a twice divorced woman. As she left the parking lot, the weight of what she'd done had made her feel like she was walking through the valley of the shadow of the death of her marriage. She was completely and totally drained of all hope that she would ever heal or love again.

By April of that year, she still wasn't motivated to get on with life. Her divorce papers arrived and she spent most of her time crying. Matt didn't even mention to her that he, too, had gotten divorce papers. She knew that he had gone on a skiing vacation at the end of March, because he told her that he wouldn't be seeing their dog for a few weeks. He came back looking tanned and rested and had all kinds of plans for the spring and summer. It was always the same things on his priority list—golfing, dragon boating, and the gym.

Lauren started going to the Friday night services at the church, and would have been relieved if the gift-giving stranger had shown up and identified himself to her. The police hadn't contacted her either to tell her that they knew who the stranger was. Everything was at a standstill, but she hadn't forgotten about him. She couldn't go out the door of her house without being acutely aware that he could be around any corner.

On the third Friday in April, she wasn't feeling well so she didn't go to the service at the church. Ever since she'd been diagnosed with fibromyalgia, she chalked up any ache or pain to the disease. Recently, every day was a struggle, and she constantly prayed that God would take her pain away. When the front doorbell rang around 9:00 p.m. that Friday evening, she went to the door without her knife and cell in her pocket. She opened the door to find a man standing there with a black toque pulled down over his forehead. She realized immediately that it had been stupid of her to fling the door wide open without at least having her knife in her pocket.

She asked the stranger what he wanted, and he told her that he was worried about her because she hadn't been at the Friday night service.

"How do you even know me?" Lauren asked.

"I watched your house being renovated," he answered. "You did a good job."

"How do you know where I live?"

"I have my ways of finding things out. Hey, I like the pink sweater you're wearing. Could I come in for a cup of tea?"

"No," she said firmly. "This isn't a good night; I'm really not feeling very well."

Suddenly it dawned on her that this stranger was Norm … Billy's friend. Norm started pacing up and down her sidewalk, and terror permeated every fiber in her body. She kept one hand on the doorknob and thanked Norm for coming by to check on her. Then she pulled the door shut and used the deadbolt to lock herself in. She was trembling so badly that she slid down to the floor. She began to beg God to protect her and tell her what she should do. She tried to calm herself down by breathing deeply, and when she could catch her breath she crawled into the kitchen and grabbed a knife. She mustered up enough courage and peeked through the blind on the door to see if he was still there. She couldn't see him in her yard, but she could see someone standing under the street light across the street and the smoke from a cigarette billowing up into the night.

What happened next could only be described as God answering her prayers. She went back to the door and yelled out, asking Norm if he was still there. He replied that he was, so she asked him to come back and talk to her for a minute. She saw him walking in her direction, and she kept praying and asking God to keep her safe.

Once Norm was in front of her, she could see that he was having trouble standing still. He turned away from her and started pacing again. In a very calm voice she told him that she thought it was very kind of him to have taken the time to stop at her house to see if she was okay. She said that sometimes it was hard for her to remember things, and she wondered if it was normal for people her age to be so forgetful. She mentioned that she just couldn't remember where she knew him from, and wondered if maybe she'd met him a long time ago. He indicated that she had, and all she could think of was to ask him if he knew her from the hospital where she used to work. He answered in the affirmative again.

Her mind was racing. "Do you remember what department I worked in?" Lauren asked.

"You were the blood lady," he told her.

"You have a great memory," she complimented him. "Were you a patient there?"

He told her that he had been a patient, so she lied and said that she remembered him from the surgical ward. Her internal dialogue sprang into action, and everything about the man came flooding back. She had taken blood numerous times from Norm when he'd been a patient on the psychiatric ward. He was always in lockup, so Lauren would have to hunt down an orderly to go with her into Norm's room. Most often he would be strapped to the bed, and the orderly would struggle trying to keep his arm still so that she could get the blood sample she needed.

Once Lauren put the Norm puzzle together, her fear turned to dread. At that moment, Norm had the power to seriously harm her. Choosing her words very carefully, she complimented Norm on his excellent memory and told him that she wished she could remember things as well as he did.

He stopped pacing long enough to say, "I remember you from twenty years ago because you were so nice to me."

When Norm stopped pacing, Lauren took the opportunity to ask him more questions. It was risky business, because she knew that at any moment he could turn on her. He seemed to like being complimented, so she used that to get his attention and then ask more questions. Keeping that in mind, she told him again how kind it was of him to go to all that trouble just to check up on her. Then she quickly asked if they had ever met any place other than at the hospital. She wasn't prepared for what he said next.

"You used to live on a lake in the south end, but then your husband left you and you moved to another lake with your new husband. He left you, too."

Lauren was stunned and struggled to ask the next question.

"Did you ever work for me at either of my homes?"

He clammed up as if he didn't know what to say.

She was painfully aware that at any time the whole situation could change and he could fly into a rage. She picked up the pace and asked question after question. She told him about the lovely gifts that been arriving at her door, then asked if while watching her home he'd ever noticed anyone on her property that looked like they didn't belong there.

He hung his head, looking bashful again, so she asked him if he was the one leaving those lovely gifts.

"Yes," he said, grinning like a Cheshire Cat.

She thanked him and told him how very thoughtful he was for remembering her during difficult times. He replied that it was his job to give people hope. She told him that because of people like him, she was doing so much better, so maybe he could start sending gifts to someone else instead.

Soon he picked up his pace and was going back and forth from the sidewalk to the street.

"I promise you that I'll never set foot on this street again," he yelled.

"Thank you so much! Just a few more quick questions, okay? What's your last name? Do you live in the same house with a guy named Billy? Do you sometimes give away pamphlets to strangers? How did you get into my house to borrow my Jesus picture? Did I meet you at my church one day when I was carrying mops and pails? Please tell me how you found out where I live?"

He walked back to her sidewalk and lit up a cigarette. "I'm Norman Weir. I live in the same house as Billy, and I don't know why you didn't recognize me, because I gave you a pamphlet one day when you drove Billy home. I have my ways of finding out where people live and how to get into their houses, because my sister works for the Governor General. Yes, that was me you met on the street in front of your church. I knew you hadn't recognized me that day." He then turned abruptly on his heels and started running down the street.

"Thanks, Norm," Lauren yelled after him. "Godspeed."

Once she was back inside her house she got down on her knees and thanked God that she was safe and now knew the identity of the stranger. The first gift from Norm had been Psalm 23. It was a fitting gift to remind her of God's presence when she did indeed walk through the valley of the shadow of death. He protected her and she didn't have to fear any evil.

29

THE KING CALLED HIM HOME
ON KING STREET

Spring turned into summer and Lauren almost forgot about Norm. She had phoned the police to give them his name. The officer she spoke to told her that they were very familiar with Norm, especially when he refused to take his psychiatric drugs. They suggested if she ever saw him hanging around her place again, she should call them right away. She assumed that Norm had forgotten all about her, because now that she knew who he was, it wouldn't be fun anymore for him to try scaring her.

That summer she started restoring furniture again—a hobby she had put on hold after Matt left. She spent many happy days stripping and sanding a piece of furniture that she knew had "good bones" underneath layers of old paint. She found a special place in her home for each piece she finished. She often reminded herself that a few people she knew had "good bones" underneath their outer layers as well. They just needed a little refinishing so that the goodness in their heart could shine through. She was sure that if they asked, God would refinish them, and they could be born again and start over.

Lauren rarely saw Matt any more, but occasionally he called to see if he could visit with the dog. Whenever she saw him, he looked and acted like he was light-years away. She didn't know if he had a new girlfriend, or if he and Jessica were an item again. There was nothing about him that she recognized anymore, except his aloofness.

He unexpectedly stopped by her home one warm and sunny day when she and the dog were in the backyard. When he opened the gate, the dog went running towards him. Matt made his usual fuss over him, and then told Lauren he had something to tell her. She pulled up a chair and told him to join her.

"I'm moving away," he said without making eye contact. "I've always wanted to know what it would be like to live out West in ski country."

Lauren immediately began to cry.

"What about your family?" she asked through her tears. "What about our nieces? What about the dog? What about your golf buddies? What about our church? You're on the counsel now. How long will you be gone, and why do you have to move thousands of miles away from your home town?"

He told her that he'd probably be gone for at least a year. With that he hugged the dog and told him he would be okay. Next he looked at Lauren, walked towards her, gave her an empty hug, and said, "See you." He walked out to his car and he was gone. He left town two weeks later with no forwarding address. Everything he did was shrouded in secrecy, which made it look like he was hiding something. When we have nothing to hide, we hide nothing.

Lauren cried for a week. It felt like her life line was gone. She had been able to count on Matt, even if for nothing else than to look after the dog if she was sick or had to go away. It had been a hard pill to swallow once he became totally uninterested in anything concerning her. If she couldn't accept the fact that he didn't care about her, she would begin to ruin what was left of her life by wallowing in self-pity and anger.

A month after Matt's departure, as she was driving down the main street in town, she saw a man on the center island waving his fists in the air and looking like he was screaming at the cars passing by. She slowed down, and when she was only a few car lengths away from him, he looked like he was going to jump out into the traffic. She couldn't slam on the brakes in case she started a chain reaction. Just when she was a few feet away from him, he stuck out his arm and stepped onto the road. She recognized him immediately. It was Norm—the gift giving stranger. She swerved to avoid hitting him head on. Once she stopped shaking, she realized that Norm must not be taking his meds, as he was acting so crazy. She decided to keep her eyes wide open for any signs of him hanging around her place.

Summer ended and Lauren still couldn't accept the fact that Matt had moved out of town. She hoped that he would soon be back and would realize that they had some work to do together if either of them wanted closure. Running away never solved anything, and she was sure he would soon come to his senses—just like the prodigal son had in the Gospel of Luke.

When she reread that story after Matt left, she had looked up the word "prodigal" in the dictionary. It was defined as "wastefully extravagant." She had always told him that it was financial suicide for him to rent an expensive apartment just so he could be alone. When she had money left over after her lake house was sold, she offered some to Matt so that he could put a down payment on a small house for himself. He had all the skills necessary if he wanted to renovate a house, and if he didn't like it after a few years, he could sell it and make money instead of throwing rent money out the window. He had turned his back on her and walked away without even thanking her for the offer.

At that time Lauren realized that he still had the power to hurt her, although she didn't know why she allowed him such power. Did she still think that she wasn't enough for him, or had he mistaken her kindness for weakness? The only way she would be able to solve that mystery was if she brought it to the Lord in prayer. From that day on she prayed daily that God would bless Matt and give him peace. At first it had been hard to do, because as bad as his betrayal had been, what he did after was even worse. Although divorced twice, she still believed in marriage and was willing to salvage whatever she could from the ashes of a marriage that had been destroyed. The only problem was that the other half of her former marriage was off enjoying life on the hills at the best ski resort in Canada.

She began to rely heavily on the words from the hymn "What a Friend We Have in Jesus." As a child, she had learned all the words to that hymn because she had heard it so often sitting beside her dad in church. The whole congregation would sing with such enthusiasm that she felt like Jesus was going to walk through the doors at any moment.

The words to that hymn seemed to cover just about everything life could throw your way. It talked about forfeiting our peace and bearing needless pain, all because we don't bring our problems to Jesus. When we are encumbered with a load of care, and even if our friends hate us and our sorrows are heavy, the answers and the healing can be found if we are willing to share them with Jesus through prayer. When Lauren finally made the choice to take not just some, but all of her problems to Jesus in prayer, her spirits lifted and she knew that no matter what Matt did or didn't do, she was not going to be willing to give him any more power to hurt her. She knew God didn't want her to give her power away to anyone that didn't respect her and want the best for her. She wrote a note and tacked it to her bulletin board. In bold letters she wrote: "I'll share my power with you, but if you try to steal all of it, I will hold you accountable, after I take it to the Lord in prayer."

Lauren also decided that she wasn't going to give Norman Weir one more ounce of power to control her by making her afraid of him. Any time she heard a strange noise in her house, she prayed for God to take her fear away. If it turned out that Norm was back, she asked God to protect her from the enemy. She still didn't know if Norm was a wolf in sheep's clothing, or if he was just a sick sheep. In her mind, one could be just as dangerous as the other.

By fall Lauren was in better emotional and spiritual shape than ever before in her life. To the best of her knowledge, Norm was staying away from her house. She started looking for a smaller home to move to and spent many afternoons driving around the city to check out neighborhoods she thought might be a suitable.

She knew all the good walking trails in the city, and often when she went shopping she would take her dog with her so that before going home they could explore a new trail. On October 1 of that year, she parked at a mall and she and her dog walked a trail that ran along the fence of a graveyard. They took a short cut on the way back to the car and walked through the graveyard. She liked reading what the tombstones had written on them. It was easy to pick out who might have been a Christian by the words on the stone. The ones she liked the best had crosses on them. Any time she was in a graveyard, she wondered how many people there had left behind unfinished business, broken promises, or unmade amends. She also wondered how many of them had died without having committed their lives to God, or how many of them hadn't believed in God?

On that fine fall day, Lauren was full of hope that she would find a suitable place to move and start all over again. Hard work never scared her, and she was willing to renovate another home just for the thrill of seeing what cleaning up and painting could do to uncover the real beauty of an older home.

As they rounded a corner in the graveyard, she had an eerie feeling that she was going to soon hear something about Norman Weir. It was odd, because she hadn't thought about him in weeks. Whenever she prayed and asked God to bless him and give him peace, she always added, "And please make sure he takes his medication."

The feeling was still with her when she returned to her car. She started the engine and turned on the radio. She was always tuned into the Christian radio station. Within minutes a news announcer came on with a report.

"The police are now releasing the name of the man who was hit by a car on King Street* yesterday."

Before the announcer said another word, Lauren said out loud, "Norman Weir."

"Norman Weir was hit and killed by a car as he was attempting to cross King Street," the announcer continued. "No charges have been laid."

Blood drained out of her face and she was sure she had goose bumps on her arms under her sweater.

"Thank you," she prayed. "Thank you, dear Lord. I don't have to worry anymore that he will hurt me. I'm not happy that he's dead, but I sure am grateful that he's gone. Please have mercy on him. Amen."

Two months later the police called her to ask if she would like to have the box of evidence back. If she didn't want it, they would destroy it. She told them that she'd be there within the next hour to pick it up. As soon as she signed the forms and the box was handed over to her, she took the lid off and looked in. When she saw the Jesus picture, she said,

"Welcome home, Jesus. You've been on quite the journey." The police officer gave her a strange look, and all she said was, "Jesus was stolen from my house, and now He's been returned. Thanks for looking after Him for me."

While driving home she sang "Jesus Loves Me" and wondered if God had given her a sign that He'd heard every word of every prayer she had ever prayed. Even the doubters in this world would have to admit that it was rather odd that the King picked King Street to call Norm home. [2]

---

[2] King Street is the actual name of the street that Norm died on. All the other names in this story are fictitious.

30

POOR ME, POOR ME

Lauren got Matt's phone number and called him on three different occasions. Each time she was in emotional and physical pain. The first time she called him was the day Karl called her from the ICU unit at the local hospital. He'd been admitted to the unit after going to the ER because of an extreme headache. He told her that he had a brain bleed and they were keeping him there for more tests.

Lauren overreacted when Karl gave her this news. The fear she felt at the mention of any brain problems was rooted in the past, because of how quickly her mother had deteriorated after brain surgery. Her brother called her not only to tell her what had happened to him, but to also tell her that he didn't want his daughters to know that he was in hospital because they would worry too much. Lauren had a fit.

"I don't have a problem doing that," she said. "But if you die do you want me to call your daughters then, or just have the hospital put you out on the curb on garbage day?"

Karl had told her that she was being ridiculous and warned her again not to call his daughters. Realizing that she was talking to one sick man, she told him that she would pray for him and that she loved him and then hung up. The pacing started shortly after. She felt like a caged animal and knew it was wrong not to let his daughters know that he was in hospital. What if he did die during the night? Would his daughters forgive their father and her for not letting them know that he was in an ICU unit?

She understood why Karl was asking this, because their father would have done the same thing. Spare the child any pain and worry. Keep them in the dark in order to avoid hurting them.

She could still remember the conversation her parents had the day her paternal grandmother died. Her mother wanted to bring Lauren to the funeral home with them, but her father was opposed—so much so that he was going to hire a babysitter for her so that she could have fun instead of being in a funeral home. She was eight years old at the time, and her father won out. She never once heard him talk about death (with the exception of Jesus' death on the cross) or pain of any kind. She had never been inside a funeral home until she was sixteen years old and her maternal grandmother had died. Her mother had won out that time.

She vividly remembered learning of her grandmother's death. When she got home from school one day, she found her mother and her three aunts sitting at the kitchen table. When she asked what they were all doing there at 2:30 in the afternoon, one of them said that her grandmother had died. Lauren started crying, but her mother stopped her.

"Stop crying," she ordered. "You're crying for yourself."

Lauren ran to her bedroom, locked herself in, and bawled her eyes out with a pillow over her head to muffle the sound.

At that funeral all the children wore new hand-stitched clothing and stood beside their parents—and nobody cried. Everybody looked good, but she didn't see one tear. As an adult, Lauren didn't begrudge them for their lack of tears, because she knew that was a learned behavior. When they were sad they felt it deeply, it just wasn't acceptable to outwardly show how they really felt. They lived what their parents had taught them, and they passed that behavior down to their children. If the circle was never broken, no one in her family would know that it was not a disgrace to cry when you were sad, and that it took courage to admit that you were hurting.

As an adult, Lauren experienced the same kind of emotional detachment from her mother. When her hair was falling out in clumps because of radiation, her mom never uttered one word about it or openly shed one tear. She was sick for eighteen years and appeared stoic at all times. Lauren always tried to hide her tears from her mother, and sometimes she locked herself in the bathroom so her mother wouldn't see her crying.

She called Matt that day because she could no longer refrain from telling someone about her brother's brain bleed. He didn't say much, except that he also thought Karl's daughters should know about their dad. When she asked him how he was, he hummed and hawed and said that the skiing was okay, but very expensive. When she asked him if was coming home soon, he gave her a "don't bug me ... I'm on the fence" answer. He never asked how she was doing, but he did ask about the dog. Lauren hung up with the familiar feeling that she must have done something to him to deserve nothing more than a cold shoulder. How was it that in her time of need, he would so easily let everything be about him? He had an uncanny way of talking about himself instead of the person who was hurting and needed support.

The second time she called him was after she moved to a smaller home. Everything had gone wrong, the sewer had been plugged for five weeks, the furnace was leaking carbon monoxide, the neighbor was giving her trouble, and everything was costing a fortune to fix.

"How are you doing?" Lauren asked.

"Once a cheater always a cheater," was his response, "and once you lose your integrity, you never get it back."

Again he had turned the tables during the conversation and made it about him. She offered to help him find a minister to talk to about forgiving himself, because she knew how important that was to his healing. She asked him if he had considered going to church, he said that he tried that once and that was it. He didn't even bother answering her when she asked about A.A. She told him that God forgives all when we ask in His name, and Matt admitted that he was trying to pray.

Those seventeen words about cheating and integrity haunted her for a very long time. All she could think about was how badly Matt must feel about being unfaithful to her, and how impossible it seemed for him to be able to overcome and forgive himself. Unknown to Lauren at that time, her feelings for Matt had more to do with feeling sorry for him than being angry at him. That's exactly where she needed to be, because her anger wouldn't give way to forgiveness, but feeling sorry for him would. The razor sharp edge of anger served no purpose in a journey of forgiveness.

The third and last time she called him was because she was in severe physical pain. After a visit to an acupuncture clinic, she had been left with peripheral neuropathy. The severe nerve pain from her knees down to the tip of her toes prevented her from sitting down for any more than a few minutes at a time, and sleeping had become almost impossible. To make matters worse, her right hand was swollen from what the doctors were calling psoriatic arthritis, and she was having difficulty using her hand. She felt like she had worked her fingers to the bone and now was suffering because of it.

She called Matt to ask if he would he take their dog if she needed surgery. She offered to pay the airfare costs of sending the dog to him. He didn't sound very happy. He told her that the dog would be okay, and then asked if there was anything more she wanted from him.

This took her totally by surprise.

"I want the truth from you," she fired back, "because the truth of what you're doing out there will set both of us free."

Nothing had changed for Mr. No Commitment. It seemed like he was getting the power he needed to control her with wishy-washy answers. Lauren's theory about him still hadn't changed. She believed that he always needed to have something to beat himself up with. If he didn't agree to take the dog, then his guilt would keep him right where he believed he should be. "I'm not enough" people go to extreme lengths to avoid commitment, because if they make the wrong choice, all they've done is validate what that little voice in their head has been telling them all along—they just aren't enough. If they continue going around the base of the mountain looking for an unoccupied fence to sit on, not only is it exhausting, but it's very painful and detrimental to their health and spirituality.

Lauren envisioned Matt at the base of a big mountain out West doing the same thing he had done at home—going around in a circle looking for someone or something to grab onto to make him feel his worth as a man. Unfortunately, we can't find or feel our worth in gyms, drinking, shopping, gambling, golfing, people, sex, romances, knowledge, bank accounts, power, drugs, or relocating, or any other worldly place.

Our personal identity and our worth are often shaped by early experiences. When we become an adult, we often still carry the same sense of worth we had as a child and teenager. In our quest to feel our worth, we can become worn-out, burned-out, frustrated, and miserable, which leads us to make what seems like an irreversible choice. The consequences of that choice can leave us in worse shape than we were before we made that life changing decision. When we see the impact of what we did, and the effect it had on the people who love us, we often can't bear the pain. We may run away, commit suicide, or live every day looking for something else with which to keep punishing ourselves.

If we don't believe in God, or we fail to turn our will and life over to Him, we will continue to look for another mountain to go around. When we keep doing the same thing, expecting different results, and nothing changes, we pick up our mountain gear and move to a different mountain. Eventually, we're so exhausted that we throw away our mountain gear and give up going around any mountain. By that time a decision has been made for us, and we believe that we are hopeless, helpless, and unlovable. We all live with what we think, and we learn to adjust our behavior accordingly. When no one wants to be around us, we validate our feelings by telling ourselves that everyone was right—we are the worst people on the face of the earth, which is why nobody wants to be associated with us.

Once we start believing that we are hopeless, helpless, and unlovable, we put ourselves in grave danger, because evil does its best work at that time. It tries to keep us right where we are. If we have weak faith or no faith at all, and don't believe that we are God's masterpiece, evil doesn't have to worry about stealing our identity. It just has to make sure that we keep that negative identity.

If we take a route that enables us to love and believe in God, evil has to work a little harder to get us back to where we can be manipulated and controlled. If we aren't marching on with the cross of Jesus before us, we'll stumble and fall. Evil often rushes in and promises us that if we stop that marching nonsense, we'll be so much better off. We'll have so much more time and money to do whatever we want, and we'll have lots of friends to do it with.

People often refuse God's love because of the guilt and shame they are carrying. If they gave into a temptation and then ran away, the time will come when they instinctively know that they should have stayed and cleaned up the mess they left behind. Their guilt will intensify daily if they don't do something about it. The longer they avoid doing the work it takes to mend broken bridges, the sicker they will get ... and Satan will laugh all the way to the warehouse where he stores his signature red uniforms with a big "S" sewn on the front.

If we don't saturate our minds with God's truth and believe that He is love and offers us a wonderful plan for our lives and for our salvation, we may end up in our casket dressed in a red suit that Satan picked out for us. By then it will be too late to undo the wrong we did while on earth and prove to God and man that we have changed because of God's love for us.

Each time Lauren spoke to Matt, she told him that real happiness comes from knowing God. She also told him that God forgives all, because we all have sinned and fallen short of His glory. Each time she managed to get a few good words out, his anger would get in the way. She felt like she was beating her head against the wall. When she asked for his forgiveness for the wrong she had done during their marriage, he didn't acknowledged her. Instead, he said that he could never come back home because she would hold his affair over his head forever. She told him that if they worked and prayed together, they could come to a place of reconciliation. That didn't mean that they would remarry, but they could at least move forward in their lives by going through the pain they shared together. Both of them could find freedom on the other side of their pain.

Matt certainly got her attention with his lack and choice of words. Often during their marriage Lauren avoided talking to him for fear that he'd get mad. He often said that she could never let anything go, and he'd been partially right. She wanted to solve the problem by talking, but Matt wanted to solve it by not talking. He preferred to bury his pain deep inside of him and refuse to share it. That hadn't changed just because he relocated and they were divorced.

31

IF YOU DON'T BUY IT,
I WILL

When Lauren was searching for a smaller home, she saw a For Sale sign on a house only minutes away from where she lived. From the outside, the house looked like it needed a tremendous amount of work, but underneath all the garbage and junk in the yard, she could see great potential. It was situated on a dead end street and had acres of undeveloped land close by. The house was brick and was covered with Virginia creeper, but the roof and windows looked fairly new. Knowing it would take time and money to restore, she called her realtor and asked to view the house.

The inside was in the same shape as the outside. It was very outdated and dirty, but Lauren could envision what it could look like if it were cleaned up and the walls were repaired and painted. The back yard was a good size for a city lot, but it had three rundown sheds. There were also many weeds and dead trees on the property. She knew it would be a challenge to turn it into a nice backyard. After she had seen everything there was to see, the realtor suggested that he call his friend who was a contractor to have a look at the house to see if it was worth renovating.

The renovator checked the place out and told her that if she didn't buy it, he would. This convinced Lauren that it must be a solid house with good potential. She knew it didn't have a basement, but the contractor looked into the crawl space and assured her that it was dry. He then told her that if she did buy the house, he had six week window of time available in which he could renovate it for her. According to the realtor, she should consider herself lucky because the contractor was one

busy man who was booked far in advance. Never once did she think
that the two men were setting her up and trying to trick her into buying
a house filled with problems just so they could make some fast money.
Even though both of her husbands had been dishonest with her, she still
believed everything she was told. She wouldn't lie to profit herself, so she
just presumed that everyone else behaved the same way.

She left the men outside talking about the cost of construction and
went back into the house by herself to have another look around. When
she was in the rundown kitchen, she bowed her head and silently asked
God to help her make the right decision. When she looked up, she
noticed a plaque with praying hands hanging on the wall. She decided
that it was a sign from above and that she would put an offer in on the
house. That plaque sealed the deal, and it would be the only thing that
didn't go into the dumpster once renovations were underway. By 10:00
p.m., her offer was accepted and she hired the contractor.

Six weeks later, on her sixty-fifth birthday, she and her dog moved
in. By then a lot of work had been done, but there still was a lot of
work to do. She had a sinking feeling when the rush and excitement
of the move was over, so she clung to those praying hands for dear life,
hoping that the plaque on the kitchen wall had been a sign from God.
On moving day, a neighbor and her teenage daughter dropped by to
welcome her and give her flowers. It was kind and generous thing for
them to do, so Lauren thanked them and told them that when she was
unpacked, she'd have them over for coffee.

During the months that followed, Lauren got to know her
neighbors. She learned that Liz, the woman who had given her flowers
on moving day, was estranged from her whole family except for her two
teenage children that lived with her. She used a cane to walk, explaining
to Lauren that she'd had surgery on her back and the doctor had messed
up, leaving her in constant pain. When she said that nobody helped her
with anything, Lauren felt sorry for her. She could empathize with the
pain, but she couldn't imagine what it must feel like not to have a family
to count on when times were tough.

Lauren's relationship with Liz and her children went fairly well for
the first year. She tried to help her neighbor whenever she could, and

Liz's daughter often brought small gifts to her as a way of thanking her. Sometimes she stayed for a short visit. Lauren never imagined anything was wrong until one day Liz said something out of the blue that surprised her.

"My daughter is always trying to defend you to me," she announced.

The only explanation Lauren could think of was that she had approached Liz one day to tell her about the mess in her yard from the old trees on the lot line. She explained to her that a huge evergreen on her property was constantly shedding needles because it was dying. Her car was always covered with brown needles, and they were embedded into the rubber around the window and had even worked their way into the engine. When she turned on her wipers, pine needles went everywhere. Every day she had to sweep or wash her driveway because of the mess from that evergreen and the old cedar trees surrounding it. She had to constantly check the eaves on her house for tree debris to make sure the water was able to drain out. Lauren offered to pay to have the dead trees on the property line removed or trimmed, but all Liz had said was, "Well, you've already cut down way too much." Then she walked away.

Since then, whenever Liz saw Lauren, she would turn her back and quickly walk away from her, or she would make some ridiculous statement and storm into her house. That cold shoulder treatment was very bothersome, because it made Lauren feel like she must have done something wrong to deserve it. Silence has a lot of power to control in a relationship when it's used as a form of punishment. If you can keep the other guy guessing and trying to figure out what exactly they did to warrant your silence, you hold the power and are able to control the relationship. If it works for bullies on the playground, why wouldn't it work for adult bullies?

From day one there had been something that just didn't feel right whenever she talked with Liz. She wasn't sure if it was a trust issue, or because she saw herself in Liz? When Liz told Lauren that she had spit on her father's grave, Lauren was able to pick up on the unresolved anger and unforgiveness. She had never spit on her father's grave, but she would admit that she still had some unresolved anger as far as Matt's affair was concerned.

She knew that "wounded people wound people," and she thought that maybe Liz had been badly wounded as a child and was still carrying a heavy burden of pain that she acted upon whenever she felt like wounding someone. If that were the case, the wrong person was taking a hit for something they had nothing to do with. That still didn't give Liz the right to treat her poorly, but it did give Lauren a chance to have a deeper understanding of what misplaced aggression looked like. That knowledge enabled her to find a place from which to start a journey of forgiveness. It's much easier to forgive someone when you feel sorry for them than trying to forgive someone when you hate them.

Although Lauren had theories as to why people acted like they did, she wasn't judging them, nor did she think she was the best counselor in the world. She wasn't trying to control them or hold the power in the relationship. Lauren believed that if she had a deeper understanding of where others were coming from and how much pain they had endured in life, she would be far more likely to have sympathy or empathy for them. Once she got to that point, her anger would diminish and she would be able to look at them in a different light. If nothing else, it would be easier to pray for them.

She believed that God put people in her path so that she could learn about herself. He was watching at all times to see how she was going to react when the people in her life didn't act the way she thought they should. Would she act wisely or foolishly? Would she act like a drunk or a grateful, sober person? Would she act like the Christian she professed to be, or would she act like she had Satan on her back cheering her on?

Big tests were on their way, and they would prove to be the tests that would make her or break her. The first test was delivered by a city by-law officer who came to her door one day and said that the neighbor to the right of her had called to complain about the fence that had just been built on her property. She said that she couldn't back out of her driveway safely because of the height of the fence. This made no sense at all to Lauren, because the neighbor's house was the last house on a dead end street with no traffic. The officer went on to say that Lauren hadn't followed the rules and regulations according to the city's by-law when she constructed the fence.

Lauren tried to explain to the officer that she had called his office many times prior to putting the fence up, and that the carpenter who had built the fence had followed the specs according to what the office had communicated. She had also spoken to her lawyer, and he had been able to provide her with an old survey that depicted exactly where the property line was. The bylaw officer successfully instilled fear in her, because he told her that she needed to take down two eight foot sections of the fence or the city would take it down for her, and she would have to reimburse the city. He also warned that if she didn't pay the bill, she wouldn't be able to sell her house until that bill was paid.

The timing couldn't have been worse. She had just survived five weeks of sewer backup, and had been so happy that day because she could finally flush the toilet. It had been a very costly job to fix and to cleanup, because the crawl space in her home was only two feet high, so whoever worked down there had to crawl on their hands and knees or roll around. The more time it took, the more money she paid out. She had a two thousand dollar deductible on sewage backup for her home, so she hadn't made a claim because she never thought the cost would exceed that, but it did. The only reason the mess got cleaned up at all was because she had been able to find a company who agreed to try to get their equipment into the crawl space through a very small trap door on the floor inside a closet.

Two middle aged women from the cleanup company had arrived at her home and somehow managed to clean and disinfect the space by crawling around on their hands and knees for hours. Lauren was sure that those women had angel wings on and had been sent from heaven above. No human being should have to endure what they did, because not only was the odor deadly, but it was extremely contaminated in the crawl space and some areas were impossible to access. At one point they asked Lauren if she had some kind of shovel that they could try to get under a cement wall that had sewage behind it. The only thing she could think of was a rake that was used to remove snow from the roof. The women figured out a way to get it behind the wall to drag the sewage out.

That wasn't the only thing that had happened prior to the by-law officer's visit. The cold air return for the furnace in her house was in the crawl space. Because of the offensive odor, she couldn't turn the furnace fan on. As a result of that, she had to redo the whole ventilation system by trying to find a way to move the cold air return to the main floor. The first company she hired ripped everything apart on the main floor and rerouted the cold air return into her bedroom. When they turned the furnace on, the decibel level was off the chart. Part of the problem was that they had busted through the cement wall between her bedroom and the furnace room on the main floor. It would have been easier to sleep in a wind tunnel than in her bed. She only had one bedroom in her home, so that all had to be changed.

She found a different company to undo what the first company had done, and they spent more time repairing the damage than they did installing a new cold air return. It wasn't perfect, but at least the noise was gone from her bedroom.

One other thing went wrong during that time. Her one year old fridge, microwave, and TV all died, and it had been an endless struggle trying to get the warranty people to come to her house to fix the problems. She kept calling them, but all she got were promises to be there as soon as they could. When the technician finally arrived at her home weeks later, he told her that he was in training, but he would try to do a good job. By the time he left, Lauren was glad to see him go, because the temperature in her supposedly repaired fridge never went below twenty degrees.

She ended up buying another fridge, but when it was delivered it didn't fit in the space in her kitchen, and the retailer wouldn't take it back. She put that fridge into the furnace room and went to a different store to buy another fridge that would fit into her kitchen.

During the sewer backup, the drain in the furnace room on the main floor backed up and left her with one big mess to clean up. She would never forget singing "Jesus Loves Me" as she cleaned up the sewage on the floor. She felt like she was having a déjà vu moment, because she had done the exact same thing thirty-five years before. After her first husband left her, the sewer had backed up in the winter because the line to the septic tank had frozen. That line ran under the garage floor, and she didn't have a clue what to do.

When she called the man who normally pumped out her septic tank, he offered to come over to help her out. When he arrived, he told her that the only thing they could do was try to trickle hot water through a garden hose into the sewage pipe in the basement. They did exactly that, and the smell of hot water and sewage mixing and flowing back in a fifty gallon can on the basement floor was enough to kill even the strongest stomach. It was hours before the ice had unthawed and the water was flowing freely.

The man refused her offer of payment, and she was convinced that day too that he had been wearing angel wings and had been heaven sent. Where would such a man come from who would be willing, out the goodness of his heart, to help a woman he barely knew unthaw a sewage line without expecting to be paid?

Lauren managed to pass the first test that the by-law officer had given her. She removed some of the boards from the fence herself because they had been screwed in. When a neighbor saw her struggling, he came by and helped her remove the rest of the boards. She left the frame standing, and what once was a beautiful fence on both sides now looked ridiculous. It was freezing outside, so she only took down one eight foot panel. To her credit, she didn't go running over to the neighbor's house to yell and scream at her for being so mean.

32

GET OFF MY PROPERTY...
YOU'RE EVIL

L auren didn't go over to her neighbor's house in a rage because she'd decided to try a different plan of attack. As angry as she was, she still remembered what Harry W. had shared with her at an A.A. meeting. He had told her that when someone hurts or wrongs him, he prays that God will bless them and give them peace. At that time she thought that would be an impossible thing to do, but since then she had read up on what the Bible had to say about what is expected of us when we are wronged. Matthew 5:44 clearly states that we are to love our enemies and bless those who curse us.

Lauren was so angry when the by-law officer told her of Liz's complaint that she felt like she was going to explode and do something stupid. She tried to calm herself by praying that God would prevent her from going next door and telling Liz what she really thought of her. She continued praying until she could feel herself calming down.

What she did next could only be described as heaven sent, and proved to her that God had heard her prayers that day. She cut out a large cross from construction paper and hung it in her bedroom window, which faced Liz's house. No more than twenty-five feet separated their homes. After that, she went to the side door that faced in the same direction, made the sign of the cross, and through clenched teeth said, "Please bless Liz and give her peace." It took a while to get the words out, and it was difficult to say, but she was proud of herself for at least trying. She faithfully said the same words in the same spot for the next month, and the anger she felt inside seemed to subside and was replaced with sympathy for Liz. She was right where she wanted to be, because if she felt sorry for her, she could forgive her, and Liz wouldn't have any more power to wound her.

Unfortunately, that was short lived. A month later the fence crew came back to finish the rest of the fence, and Liz's anger surfaced again. Lauren cautioned the workers to be very careful that they didn't step over the property line or leave anything, not even a small rock, on the neighbor's land. She constantly checked to make sure that Liz wouldn't have a reason to complain again. When she went into the house to talk to a furnace tech who was working on her furnace, Liz struck again. She must have been watching from a window, because once Lauren went inside, she came over.

When Lauren went back outside, one of the young men digging the holes for the fence posts told her that they'd had a visitor. He told her that the woman from next door had maneuvered her way through the long grass to get to them and swung her cane at them, warning them to respect the property line. Lauren went wild, because she had told Liz that if she had a problem that concerned her, all she had to do was talk to her and they could try to resolve the problem. The fact that she had snuck over and tried to induce fear into the young men working on the fence made her livid. The only humor she could find in the whole situation was the mental image of a cartoon caption depicting a person wielding a cane at someone and demanding respect. Did Liz have any right to talk about respect when she wasn't exhibiting any? Respect is earned, not dished out by threatening someone.

All hope of asking God to bless Liz went out the window that day. Lauren reverted back to her stinking thinking days and fired off a letter to Liz, telling her that she wasn't okay with her swinging her cane at the young men who were working on her property. If she had a problem, all she had to do was talk to her. She needed to leave innocent bystanders out of whatever battle she was fighting. Other people didn't need to take a hit because of her misplaced aggression. She made a few other rude comments then quickly sealed the letter and ran it over to Liz's mailbox.

By the time she got back to her house, she started to feel guilty. She tried convincing herself that Liz was a wolf in sheep's clothing, and she wanted nothing to do with her. When her guilt persisted, she began to wonder who was convicting her. Was the Holy Spirit convicting her to push her away from the ensnarement of sin, or was a condemning spirit working in her to push her away from God by making her feel guilt and shame?

After thinking things over, she decided that it wasn't worth the risk to do nothing, so she wrote another letter to Liz asking for her forgiveness. She told her that she couldn't walk around saying she was a Christian and an alcoholic in recovery if she wasn't going to act like one. In her letter she included a gift of a tree donation that said that a tree would be planted for her in a special place in their city. It was her way of proving that she was serious about her apology. She put that letter in Liz's mailbox and waited to see if there would be any kind of hint from her that she was willing to accept that apology. When nothing happened, she took it upon herself to go over to see Liz and try to talk to her.

She was met with anger and hatred unlike anything she had ever seen before. Lauren tried to tell her that she was serious about the apology. She also told her that one day she would be held accountable for the role she played in relationships, so it was important to her to apologize before she was placed in a coffin. She didn't want to be holding hatred in her heart when she left this earth. Liz just shook with rage. Her words cut like a two edged sword.

"Get off my property," she screamed. "You're evil!"

Lauren retreated and went home. All she could think about was the damage that words can do. When two edged swords are misused, the wielder can get badly cut or killed as easily as the person being attacked. Two weeks prior to Liz's verbal attack, Lauren had listened to one of her favorite ministers speak on what to do when an apology isn't accepted. He said that the important part of apologizing is knowing that we do it for ourselves so that we don't hinder our relationship with God. In Matthew 6, Jesus instructs us to forgive those who have wronged us, because He forgives us when we ask in His name. Lauren understood that to mean that if she refused to forgive Liz, or Matt, or anyone else, God would not forgive and bless her. It was a small price to pay in order to receive forgiveness from God for her many sins.

The minister had gone on to say that once you sincerely ask a person to forgive you, whether they accept your apology or not, you have done your part. When they refuse, you simply hold forgiveness in your heart for them, knowing that you tried to fix the broken bridge between you. Lauren liked that part, because for her it meant that once she held forgiveness in her heart for her neighbor, Liz would have no more power to hurt her again. The ball was in Liz's court after that.

After being called evil, Lauren hit rock bottom and asked God to guide and heal her. It wasn't long before Nicole, the neighbor on the other side of her who claimed to be a friend of Liz's, started her own campaign to hurt her. One day she called Lauren over to have a little chat with her. She said that Liz was very distraught and couldn't stop crying because Lauren had been so mean to her. Liz had had her lawyer over and then called Lauren over to give her a lecture on diligence.

After that episode, a few more things happened. Nicole seemed to be fixated on a small decorative fence that divided their properties. She asked Lauren twice if she would mind if she painted it, and Lauren always responded the same way. She told her that she believed that the fence wasn't on her property, so Nicole could do whatever she wanted with it. The third time Nicole asked, Lauren said that if it was that important to her, she would find the original owner of her house and ask him whose fence it was. Lauren knew she was coming across as rude and that bothered her, so a week later she went to see Nicole and apologized to her. She then tried to defend herself by saying that it hadn't been necessary for Nicole to give her a lecture on due diligence, because she'd been raised in a home that taught their children all about due diligence and how important it was to treat their neighbors well.

Nicole claimed that she'd intended no harm. Lauren told her that she knew that, but what she didn't tell her was that what she saw was a woman making a feeble attempt to let her friend, Liz, know that she would save her from having to cry and worry about her mean neighbor. A few months prior to that incident with Nicole, Liz had told her that she considered Nicole's new live in boyfriend to be the enemy. Just when their friendship had been going strong, Nicole had gone and gotten herself a boyfriend because she really needed a man. Lauren remembered wondering why Liz would call herself a friend if she wasn't happy for Nicole. There was a real possibility that Lauren had taken a hit because Nicole was trying to impress her friend to make up for not spending as much time with her anymore. Lauren asked herself if she wanted to continue living in the middle of two women she didn't trust.

Before moving to that house, Lauren had been diligent in her prayer life. She kept asking for the wisdom to know if it would be a good move for her to make. After three years in the house, she understood why God had placed her there. She needed to look at a mirror reflection of herself in her neighbors to see what it looked and felt like to hurt people with her words and actions. Our thoughts about others provide us with a perfect reflection of how we feel about ourselves. We are all mirrors for each other. We hate others when we hate ourselves. We forgive others when we forgive ourselves, and the most important thing we do is love others when we love ourselves.

If we want to be a reflection of God's love, we only need to look into a mirror of a neighbor's face. What does that look like? Are we loving or hating our neighbor like ourselves? If we see hate, we are destined to live with hate in our heart and act accordingly by trying to destroy our neighbor and, ultimately, ourselves. If we see love, we will treat our neighbor with love and prove that we are trying to be a good reflection of God's love for us by setting an example of what love looks like.

33

THESE TRIALS ARE TOO MUCH FOR ME

With all of the nonsense going on around her, Lauren became extremely upset because she felt like the whole world was against her. Everybody had turned their back on her. Now she was trapped between two women who were friends, and both of them seemed to be out to get her. For the first time in her life, she questioned God and asked Him what she had done that was so terrible that she deserved to be treated poorly. Wasn't it enough that both of her husbands had abandoned her, and she had worked and prayed hard to survive the consequences of those betrayals? Wasn't it enough that she had learned how to forgive both of them so that she could be forgiven? Hadn't it been enough that she had tried to help Liz and her children when she was in severe emotional and physical pain herself? Hadn't it been enough that she was constantly sending Matt encouraging words and letters to try to help him heal, and in return got nothing but a cold shoulder? What more did He want from her?

Her prayers had not been in vain. Soon her spirits lifted and pieces of the puzzle began to fit together. God made it crystal clear to her that she needed to keep looking into the mirror that would reflect what was in her heart, and she needed to stop trying to own what others did and blame herself for how they acted. They were responsible for what they did, and one day they would be held accountable for it. She would never be asked to account for what Matt, Doug, Liz, Nicole, or anyone else did; however, she would be held accountable for what she had done. On judgment day, when the Book of Life was opened, there would be no more second chances. If her name wasn't in the book, she would never hear the words from Matthew 25:21: "*Well done, thou good and faithful servant!*" If she heard the words from Matthew 7:23, "*I never knew you: depart from me …*," she would have no one to blame but herself.

If she wasn't trying to live the best she could in preparation for meeting her Lord and Savior on Judgment Day, she had a lot to worry about. If she put her foolish pride, selfishness, envy, and greed first in her life, then she needed to take some crash courses in forgiveness, amends, gratitude, love, peace, and humility—considering that three-quarters of her life was already over and time was running out.

She couldn't try blaming her parents for never telling her about God, because they had raised her in the church. They were God fearing people who loved her and her siblings, and made sure that all four of them knew about God and were grateful for His blessings. They led by example by being very active in the church. Her dad had taught Sunday school and contributed in many other ways to the growth of the church. Her mother had been extremely active in the women's groups, and most of her friends and her sister were members of the same church and were constantly organizing events like picnics or bake sales. They made sure that everyone was invited to join in and celebrate and have some fun. They were a strong group of women who worked without complaint so that their families could understand how important it was to part of a church family.

They may not have been the best at talking about feelings, but in the big scheme of things, the lessons her parents taught their children were irreplaceable. Feelings don't get us to Heaven, but our faith does. If her parents hadn't laid the ground work to give her a place from which to start her journey of faith, she was sure that she would have taken a different road. There was no doubt in her mind that she'd be in jail or a graveyard.

Children live what they hear and see their parents do. If a parent is an atheist, chances are their child will be one, too. If a father or mother commits adultery, chances are greater that their adult son or daughter will do the same thing. If a child has a father who walks around puffing on a big cigar and swinging a stick at everyone, swearing and demanding respect, chances are that without intervention and prayer, the adult child will not respect anyone either.

If Lauren tried to blame her ex- husbands, or her infertility, or her alcoholism, or her toxic neighbors for not making God her first priority in life, she worried that on Judgment Day God may say, "So what? I carried you through all those hard times and you learned a lot more about suffering and being able to endure through hard times than you would have if your life had been perfect." She also couldn't use her physical or emotional pain as an excuse, because at nearly sixty-nine years of age she was still self- sufficient and could do whatever she wanted to do. She still had a home and a pension, and she knew many who were not able to look after themselves and didn't have a pension that allowed them to have proper housing, good food, or the meds they needed.

Just about every excuse she could think of for not putting God first in her life was just a feeble attempt to try to justify herself. Her life was going to end one day, and if she chose to ignore all the biblical warnings, she would be thrown into a lake of fire. Thinking about that possibility scared her silly. She avoided even trying to conjure up a mental image of what that might look like. What scared her even more was the thought of the people she loved that didn't believe in God and had made no preparation for life after death. That would be such a great tragedy that could have been avoided. If only they'd believed in God and tried to act like it while on this earth. She didn't own that one either, and couldn't make them believe in God, but what she could do was pray for them.

God had blessed her in so many ways that it just didn't seem right to whine about her life or "poor me" herself to death. She'd tried that for a while, but it only made her sicker. She couldn't stand being her own worst enemy. Her unwarranted anger and her unforgiving spirit made her sicker, and she looked like some eighty year old woman who was weathered, homeless, and mad at the world.

Getting out of herself was difficult, but when she put others first, she shone and was sure that she was a good reflection of God's love. When she was stuck feeling sorry for herself and acting hateful and mean and whining and complaining, she was sure that she was a good reflection of Satan's character.

The best thing to happen to her was to know in her heart that she had forgiven Matt and that she didn't hate him or want to harm him in any way. She believed it would have been easier for him if she was constantly beating him up for being a bad boy, since he seemed to need to live in a state of self-hatred. After knowing the man for thirty years, she felt like she had insight into his much guarded secrets and pain. All she had was a gut feeling about him, but she would admit she was wrong if he ever tried to prove to her that he was sorry for hurting her so badly.

Lauren would forever have an image in her mind of a man tethered to a chain that was attached to a boulder. If he was strong enough and could pick up the boulder and carry it everywhere he went, his back would eventually break. If he didn't believe that God held the key to unlock every heavy weight we drag through life, then he would be taking that boulder with him to his grave.

In her attempt to help Matt, Lauren mailed him a Bible. Inside she put a note telling him to read the story of David and Bathsheba in 2 Samuel, and to read Ephesians 4:3–32. She wanted him to know that the greatest weapon God had given believers was forgiveness. By forgiving, we slam the door shut against demonic forces and stop the harm being done to us. We also set ourselves free from carrying a heavy burden in our heart.

Lauren once told her minister that she believed that adultery was the most difficult sin to overcome and forgive. In 1 Corinthians 6:18, we are told to flee from sexual immorality. All other sins a person commits are outside the body, but whoever sins sexually, sins against their own body. Her minister agreed with her that it was a very serious sin against our own body.

34

THE POWER OF LOVE
OVERCOMES THE POWER OF FEAR

It took Lauren years before she completely understood how detrimental it was to live with a shadow of fear hanging over her head. Oddly enough, it was her father's lack of words to her the day her brother Warren had been born that would change the course of her life. Her dad hadn't stopped loving her, but in her eight year old mind it felt like she had been replaced by her brother. This scared her, because she thought that her dad didn't love her anymore. In reality, that hadn't been the truth. Nothing had changed as far as her father was concerned, but she had changed and started to act differently. She wasn't a happy-go-lucky kid anymore, but was always helping out and trying to be the best child possible in order to win her father's love back. He hadn't kicked her off the pedestal—she had jumped off to make room for her brother.

After solving this "puzzle," Lauren went to the graveyard to talk to her father. She stood at his grave, looked towards the heavens, and told him that on the day her brother was born, she had felt like he didn't love her anymore. She now understood that was not the case. Her emotions had been a little mixed up when she was eight years old. She then thanked him for loving her right to the end, and told him that she could hardly wait to see him again. She had so many stories to share and looked forward with anticipation to being with him, her mother, and sister in heaven. He had been the one who taught her not to worry or be afraid, because God was looking after her, just like He looked after the sparrows in the field. She had never forgotten that lesson. Even as an adult, she would imagine God swooping down from heaven and picking her and a wounded sparrow up to protect them until their fear subsided.

When she left the graveyard that day, she felt lighter. It was as if she had dropped off a heavy burden. Her future looked brighter, and her fears had been calmed. Her father's legacy for her was that he was the first one to teach her about God and give her hope that she didn't have to live with fear in her heart. She was sure that there was no better legacy a father could leave for his child. She could envision God saying to him, "Well done my good and faithful servant."

Once she understood her core issue, she became gentler with herself. She was aware of how fortunate she had been to have good parents who, just like her, had a few character defects. No one in her family had done anything to her with the intent to harm her, and she was filled with gratitude for the family she'd been born into.

When she thought about her ex-husbands, there was no doubt in her mind that her prayers for guidance and wisdom had been heard and answered. She had treated both of them fairly after the initial shock of their betrayal wore off. She hadn't taken either of them to court, or tried to bleed them dry. Eventually she prayed for God to bless them and give them peace. The best part was that she could feel the power of God's love working in her through her pain, and she knew that the hope God's love had given her would carry her into eternity if she kept on believing.

As an added bonus, she was able to let Doug and Matt own what they had done. Just like everyone else, she was flawed, full of pride, and prone to making mistakes. She believed that she had nothing to do with the choices both men had made to have an affair. It was about them, not her. She owned half the marriage, but she didn't own any part of their affairs, and would never be held accountable for what they had done.

Their behavior was typical of people who betray their spouses. They lie and sneak around and give the devil permission to use them as a pawn. They have no insight into the consequences of the harm they are causing others, because their priority is themselves. When they don't follow through on their wedding vows, they break a promise to God and their spouse. Their integrity takes a big hit, and it's impossible to restore without God's forgiveness and help.

Once the "for better" part ends and the "for worse" part begins, they leave and try to find another woman so that they can have another "for better" part. They convince themselves that there will never be a "for worse" part, because the new woman is so right for them. Lauren didn't think that her ex-husbands were bad men, or that she was better than them, but their choices had far reaching, detrimental effects on them and their families. She also knew that God still loved them, and that if they wanted forgiveness and sanctification, it was there for the asking through faith, just like it was there for everyone else.

Not only did Lauren feel the power of God's love working in and through her, but she also felt the power of fear weakening and losing its grip on her. The more she felt God's love, the less afraid she felt. Fear had the most power over her when she was hungry, angry, lonely, tired, and sick. She was consumed with "what if" questions. What if I can't look after myself and my dog? What if I can't look after my house and have to pay someone to cut the grass and shovel? What if the sky falls in? What if I run into my ex-husband and his girlfriend in the grocery store? What if he marries her? What if I have to move because I can't continue to live beside a woman who called me evil? What if she tries to poison my dog or runs him over to get back at me? The questions nearly drove her insane. One day her doctor told her that she was concerned about her mental health. Lauren replied that she was worried, too. Now she asked: "What if I 'what if,' myself right into a mental institution?"

Whenever she was in severe physical pain, or felt afraid, she called Matt. She eventually realized that every time she talked to him, she felt more pain. Even when she asked him to take the dog, he hadn't said that he would. She could picture him teeter tottering on a fence, trying not to fall off. When she begged him for help, she was met with that dreaded silence she hated. That translated into more stress, more pain, and more fear. Why did she keep asking him for help when he had made it very clear to her that he either couldn't or wouldn't help her?

Without the power of God's love for her, she wouldn't have survived. Pain made her crazy, and the best and only way she found to deal with it was to take one of her many crosses to bed with her and hang on tightly. She'd chant over and over again, "Please, dear Lord, heal me, if it is your will." A miracle seemed to happen when she gave her pain to God. It wasn't that all her pain was gone, but it felt like she was less afraid. That always proved to be the best medicine for her. Less fear equaled less pain.

The more fear she carried with her, the more "what if I can't" consumed her. The more she surrendered her pain and her life to God, the less afraid she was. The less afraid she was, the better she felt. The more she prayed for Matt and Liz, the less afraid she was of them. She understood that she was the one who had given them the power to hurt her. They could still try, but it wouldn't be as effective, because by that time in her life she had given her life over to God, believing that He was protecting her from them. By asking God bless both of them, she lost her anger at them and could live her life with transparency. She did her best to apologize, yet neither of them had the decency to acknowledge her. She still carried forgiveness in her heart, just in case if they ever decided to look her in the eye and talk to her. She was right where she wanted to be.

After she'd returned home from the treatment center she promised herself that one day she would to prove to God her eternal gratefulness that He had chosen to send her a messenger of His to deliver a card to her that would change the course of her life forever. The instructions on that card were to trust in the Lord with all her heart, and not to lean on her own understanding. If she acknowledged Him in all her ways, He would direct her path.

God had done exactly what He'd promised. He never failed or stopped loving her; He never disappointed or abandoned her, and He had stood at every intersection of every road she had taken to show her which way to go. Sometimes she had ignored him and driven around in circles, but because of Him, she had eventually been able to get back onto the straight and narrow road that led to the peace that passes all understanding. There was no doubt in her mind that she wasn't taking any hostages into her coffin with her. If she could carry those lessons with her for the time she had left on this earth, she would have a good chance of hearing, "Well done, my good and faithful servant."

By forgiving others and making amends, she could live her life without worrying that she had neglected to ask for or give forgiveness.

The ones she had asked to forgive her who had ignored her would never be free of her, because they were still carrying the anger they felt towards her in their hearts. Those people had been excellent teachers, because they had unknowingly taught her more about herself than she could ever have hoped. She now understood why God hadn't removed them from her life when she had asked Him to. She had needed a mirror reflection of herself to look into so that she could see herself more clearly.

She could feel God's love for her more than at any other time in her life, and the unhealthy fear she had been carrying around for sixty years was finally gone. It had been replaced with these words from 2 Timothy 1:7: *"For God has not given us a spirit of fear, but of power and of love and of a sound mind"* (NKJV). Amen!

Testimonial of My Faith

I struggled when trying to write a testimonial of my faith, even though I didn't seem to have a problem writing 62,000 words about my life and all the signs that God had given me as proof that He loves me unconditionally. I tried numerous times to write down what was it about me that would prove that I was a grateful Christian and I try to act like one by living my life accordingly.

In order to solve my dilemma, I prayed for discernment and wisdom. As always, God heard my prayers, and I thank Him for reminding me of the words to Hymn #370 in my Lutheran hymnal. It's amazing that at my age I can still remember all the words to "On Christ the Solid Rock I Stand." I heard that song almost every Sunday when I was a child sitting beside my parents in the Lutheran church.

The hymn corresponds to 1 Timothy 1:12–13. The Apostle Paul is traditionally identified as the author of this book. It appears as if Paul hadn't always worked for God.

I thank Christ Jesus our Lord, who has given me strength, that he considered me trustworthy, appointing me to his service. Even though I was once a blasphemer and a persecutor and a violent man, I was shown mercy because I acted in ignorance and unbelief. (NIV)

My testimony mirrors those words from Paul. I thank Christ Jesus who has given me strength to endure the trials and tribulations in my life by appointing me to His service. I was once an angry alcoholic, twice divorced, abandoned woman who thought that the world owed me. Jesus showed me mercy, because I acted in ignorance and unbelief. The Lord poured grace out on me abundantly, along with the faith and love that are in Jesus Christ.

My hope is built on nothing less than Jesus blood and righteousness. On Christ the solid rock I stand, because people and worldly things have failed and disappointed me. God has had to pull me out of sinking sand many times in my life. He has calmed every storm and has been an anchor for me by carrying and loving me unconditionally.

I have a strong desire to leave behind a legacy that speaks to my love and gratitude to Christ Jesus. I believe that my job on earth has been, and will continue to be, to pay my story forward in hope that there is someone out there who will feel God's unfailing love and acceptance, and be able to live a changed life out of gratitude.

It was no accident that I was chosen by God to receive a card while in a drug rehab program that would inspire to keep moving forward and to be grateful enough to act like the Christian I proclaim to be. There is nothing better in life than knowing in your heart that you are living the way God intended you to, and that He is working in and through you to bring others home to Him.